S heilds realised he'd been staring into the darkened streets for several minutes, becoming lost in his thoughts, in all those faces which'd be forever scared onto his mind's eye; the twisted faces of those who he had killed.

Sometimes he didn't quite understand what came over him.

Sometimes he wished there might be a cure for whatever it was that he had.

In the Kingdom of Shellacnass,
a decade of peace passes by.

But all it brings is a sense of foreboding.

With ice magic in her veins, Syre Dorf feels this
more than most.

That great danger lingers in the shadows.
Ready to destroy everything all over again.

If Syre chooses to stand by and do nothing.

An action-packed fantasy adventure.

CROW'S MIND

THE FOURTH CRYSTAL KINGDOM NOVEL

- RAYMOND S FLEX -

books

Crow's Mind

ISBN-10: 1-78532-025-4

ISBN-13: 978-1-78532-025-5

Published by DIB Books, 2015.
www.dibbooks.com

THE CRYSTAL KINGDOM SERIES

The Webbing Trilogy

The Webbing Blade
The Webbing Bow
The Webbing Cloak

The Four Corners Quartet

Crow's Mind
Heart of Flame
Galleries of Justice
Hitchking

Collections

Blood & Guts & Hexes

CROW'S MIND

THE FOURTH CRYSTAL KINGDOM NOVEL

- RAYMOND S FLEX -

HOMECOMING

S heilds could feel the chill of the night air against the back of his neck. It crept in beneath the collar of his sable traveller's cloak. He could feel the chill up against his bald scalp which he'd freshly shaved that morning using the head of a Royal Guard's spear.

Any moment now, the snow would begin to tumble down. Ice would form beneath his feet, covering the cobblestones. And the night-time fog would descend.

Winter.

Winter again.

No longer did the curse remain over the city, from what Sheilds had heard, and, indeed, he hadn't run into any cursed animals on his way here.

On his way, here, to Ilsnare: the Crystal City.

Sheilds's mouth tasted stale and his heart beat infrequently, and weakly. He hadn't had anything of substance to eat since he had left Shildersmoore—since he had got free of the prison colony of Onderswort.

That had been weeks ago, or had it been months now?

He had lost track of all time.

Since he had had no money to spend on transport, let alone food, he had made his way here on slit throats and twisted necks.

Those same crimes which'd seen him sent to Onderswort had brought him back.

It was hard to believe that he actually stood here, in the well-swept, cobblestone streets; and that he'd made it back here, to Guider Street, to this very door . . . to what had been his childhood home.

Why he had come here, he really hadn't much of an idea. Perhaps because it was the only place in the whole Kingdom which seemed *familiar* to him.

He glanced up the street, past the flickering torches, shedding their orange glow about the night-time city. Up on one of the roofs, he spotted a crow. One of its beady eyes considered him for a moment, and then, as if Sheilds had somehow spooked it, the bird flapped its wings and soared gracefully up and away, into the air.

Sheilds smiled to himself.

For some reason, animals always seemed to recognise him for what he was.

In the near distance, Sheilds could hear the croaky *whine* of strings—a group of minstrels. And, a little way beyond them, he could hear the throaty singing of pub-dwellers.

It would be so easy for Sheilds to slip through these darkened streets, to arrive outside the tavern and to lurk in the shadows, waiting for one of those drunkards to emerge, sozzled in brandy wine or ale. From the way most drunkards' pockets clinked as they trudged along, Sheilds was certain that he would find it worth his time.

When the night-time fog settled in over the streets, it would be the perfect cover.

Sheilds realised he'd been staring into the darkened streets for several minutes, becoming lost in his thoughts, in all those faces which'd be forever scared onto his mind's eye; the twisted faces of those who he had killed.

Sometimes he didn't quite understand what came over him.

Sometimes he wished there might be a cure for whatever it was that he had.

But it was too late to think about all of the *should-haves*, and *would-haves*; because he was a hardened killer well beyond his fortieth summer in the Kingdom of Shellacnass.

Redemption, whatever that might really mean, was for monks.

Feeling his blood cool, and his mind quiet—*calm*—Sheilds brought his fist up to the weathered, familiar door, and beat a pair of percussive, decisive, knocks.

ACROSS TOWN

It was a bitter, foul, winter's night.

The snow tumbled down like freshly plucked cotton. But, unlike cotton, its feel wasn't warm or soothing, it was cold and alien. Impossible to stand for too long of a time.

The wind whipped in through the narrow, cobbled streets, and only one of every four torches remained lit; and those which did remain lit were never more than a flicker away from being snuffed out by the unending gales.

Syre Dorf could feel her whole body seize up with shaking. She bundled the thick, sheepskin cloak tighter about her. Although she had cloaks of her own, she preferred to take those which belonged to her brother when she went out at night. They were bulkier, and served to better hide her womanly form. To make her seem as if she was a travelling merchant leaving with the daylight, headed back to whichever provincial town she had left that morning.

Her brother—Louson, the King of Shellacnass—wouldn't miss the cloak because he almost never left the Palace. Indeed, he almost never even left his quarters. Just about the only person who he ever admitted was Syre herself.

She worried about him desperately, and she had tried in vain to make him more sociable, to have him shrug off the dark cloud which constantly lingered above his head.

But, now, ten years into his reign as King of Shellacnass, Syre had resigned herself to the fact that there was nothing to be done for Lou.

That she had done her best and been unable to change his mind.

Already she had wasted the remainder of her childhood in trying to do that, and now it was *her* turn to live her own life for a change.

And that was what had brought her here tonight.

To this shady back alley, encrusted with a beautiful, virginal layer of snow.

But which still stank of rat piss.

As Syre eyed up the door before her, she could still taste the chicken broth she had consumed an hour before. Despite the House Staff's best efforts, and their butler—Tineoots—attempting to have Syre act more 'ladylike', Syre refused to eat anywhere else but the kitchens of the Palace.

Since her brother had taken to the throne through force, rather than through any sort of a bloodline, Syre's position throughout the royal household was hardly etched into stone. She supposed that Tineoots's attempts to have her act as if she was a princess, eat on her own in one of the banquet rooms, with servants attending to her, was meant to serve the argument that she should be the one to inherit the throne if her brother died without heir.

But Syre had no intention of inheriting the throne.

Quite the opposite, she was determined to leave Ilsnare.

Oh, she understood that Tineoots, like all other citizens of Ilsnare, was deeply afraid of the city descending into madness and tyranny if anything did happen to Lou, but Syre herself could hardly raise any sense of sympathy for the fate of Ilsnare.

She hadn't been born here like the others.

Quite frankly, she wouldn't care less if it burned to the ground.

She eyed the large, oak door which darkened the wall of the alleyway; looked to the pairs of barrels which rested beside it. Their lids were left ajar, and Syre could see that nothing remained within either of the barrels. But she still caught the pungent stench of ale which wafted out from within. It was like Midwinter's Day when she would enter the kitchens. That stench would linger on every servant's breath; even Tineoots's.

As she drew closer to the door, she wondered if she should knock, but, first, she decided to see if it was bolted. She reached out, turned the handle.

And it gave.

She glanced back over her shoulder and then slipped inside.

As Syre brought the door shut behind her, she savoured the warmth for several moments. She felt the feeling return to her cheeks, and then flood down her neck, to her chest.

Last of all, the feeling returned to her fingers.

She glanced about her, realising that she stood in darkness.

Before she had believed the streets to be dark—there was no moon tonight and a quarter of the torches throughout the city had been blown out—but now she had entered a far more profound level of darkness. When she took a step forward, she couldn't entirely shift the idea that she might be about to take a tumble down into a bottomless pit.

Instead, though, she felt the insistent point of a dagger at her stomach.

"Evenin', stranger," the dagger owner said. "Took a wrong turn, have ya?"

Syre felt her body stiffen. Her heart fluttered in her throat. She stared into the gloom, attempting to make sense of the shapes before her, but the darkness seemed to swirl together, to be impossible to separate into any kind of rational order.

"I'm here for the meeting," Syre said, keeping her voice firm and even.

She listened to the hitch of the dagger owner's breath, could smell the stench of onions and garlic. It almost made her want to double over and retch . . . and wouldn't that be just the very thing for a *princess* to do?

"Meetin'," the dagger owner said, "What meetin'?"

Syre felt a fresh wave of cold pass through her veins. Her mind switched back to the information she had overheard from the wise woman, at the market, a week earlier. The wise woman had spoken about the Outcast meeting; about the address, here, the entrance at the back alley of *The Soore Whip*, a public house which Syre had had the good fortune of avoiding thus far in her residency in Ilsnare.

The woman's conspiratorial tone had intrigued her.

"I was . . ." Syre finally uttered.

Syre felt the dagger press harder into her stomach.

She knew that it would take some severe force for the dagger to pierce through the sheepskin cloak, but neither was she in the mood to test the theory.

". . . the *Outcast!*" she finally got out, feeling the dagger press harder still.

The dagger remained where it was for several seconds, and then she felt it retreat from her. She listened to the dagger owner's ragged breathing, could feel the warmth emanating from his body.

She wondered how close he was to her.

Close enough to reach out and touch, at the very least.

"What are ya?" the dagger owner said.

"What?" Syre replied.

The dagger owner drew another few forceful breaths, then exhaled with a shuddering force. "You Mortal?"

Syre felt her throat tighten, and she realised that she had no other option. First she nodded, and then, remembering the darkness, and that the dagger owner couldn't see her, she replied, ". . . Yes."

More heavy breathing from the dagger owner, and Syre wondered if he might be about to draw a more deadly weapon, or call for assistance.

Syre was fairly certain that, if it came down to it—if she *really* had to protect herself—then she would be able to stand her ground. After all, just like her brother, she had ice magic flowing through her blood. And, what was more, she had a certain 'gift' for dark magic . . . if *gift* was how it could be termed.

"Sympathiser?" the dagger owner finally got out.

Syre considered this, absorbed the dagger owner's tone, and decided that she had better respond in the affirmative. "Yes," she said, "that's right."

A long pause—one of those pauses which, the longer it existed, made Syre intently believe that she might feel the dagger slit her throat.

But then the dagger owner said, "Go on through."

Unable to quite believe it, Syre blinked away her daze, and then stepped away from the dagger owner, treading deeper into the darkness. She had only got half a dozen steps when she felt the dagger owner take hold of the sleeve of her cloak.

His lips—*dry and scabbed*—brushed up against her earlobe. "I'll be keepin' my eye on you, stranger, so dontcha try anything, understand?"

Syre nodded that she did, and then, after another few moments, the dagger owner let her go.

THE OUTCAST

S yre was hit by a cacophony of smells as she trod on in through the doorway, to the room which glowed with the flickering orange light of torches. She breathed in the musky scent of body odour, mixed in with dung and ale.

But the most prevalent of them all was the stench of rotten eggs.

It wasn't since she'd been a child back in Endmere, or while she'd been living in an encampment in the foothills of the Sable Mountains, that she had found herself so bowled over by smell.

The room was kept in gloom, and, as she stepped forward, she felt the exposed floorboards giving way beneath her feet. She found herself among bundled-up bodies, all of them—*like her*—wearing hooded cloaks as much to protect their anonymity as to guard against the cold outside.

There must've been thirty, or forty, people.

It was a back room of the pub, and she could see that a rickety stage had been erected near the front, where a trio of torches hung from the wall, burning away.

Off to the side of the stage, she could make out another few figures.

Five of them.

They *too* were wrapped in their winter cloaks.

Hoods drawn down.

She could hear all manner of languages coming at her from all sides. She had only, in the last few years, begun to converse fluently in the Ilsnare dialect; and she couldn't hear so much as an uttering of it among this crowd.

She supposed that the languages being spoken came from all over Shellacnass.

There was so much to learn in this world, and here she was, cooped up in the Palace with her dour brother, while all those experiences outside the walls of the Crystal City lay in wait.

She felt an itchy sensation down the back of her neck—the ice magic irritating her veins. A sensation which she had learned to interpret as somebody watching her without her knowledge.

Sure enough, when she turned to look, she saw that the dagger owner stood in the doorway to the room. Like all the others who surrounded her, he wore a cloak. His face remained in shadow from beneath the hood.

As Syre caught him staring at her, she thought that she spotted the light reflecting off the surface of his eyeballs.

Something about the sight disquieted her, but she tried not to think too much about it.

She knew enough about skulking around in the shadows that, if one was to remain undiscovered, they needed to do so without raising suspicion.

And that meant not making an impact on others.

It meant *not* arousing suspicion in others.

She turned back to face the rickety stage, and where she could see the cloaked figures breaking from their huddle. One of them trod forward to the front of the stage while the other four all remained at the back.

When the first speaker raised his—*her?*—voice, it was full of force, and resonated all about the tight little room. "Brothers and sisters, welcome to tonight's meeting—the *thirteenth* meeting of the Outcast."

The speaker spoke in the Ilsnare dialect, but with an accent far stronger than Syre's own.

Syre turned her attention to those surrounding her.

She could hear some of them muttering words beneath their breath.

In their own languages.

Languages which Syre hadn't a hope of understanding.

If only she had more experience of the world—perhaps if she had left behind the protective walls of Ilsnare, ventured out to have her own adventures; just like her brother, Lou, had had his own.

Perhaps then she would be just as jaded as he was now.

The speaker at the front of the stage went on to talk about the 'furthering of the cause' and the 'fightback against unjust treatment', but, as far as Syre was concerned, it might as well have been in a foreign tongue.

Because she couldn't comprehend a word.

What was this all about?

She found herself glancing back over her shoulder once more, to the dagger owner who stood in the doorway to the back room. Once more, she caught that reflection from within his hood, that *glint* as the torchlight met with the surface of his eyeballs.

When she turned back to the front, she realised that the speaker, and those cloaked figures lurking behind, had all bowed their heads, and that they were chanting in some language, *unknown* to Syre.

Reminding herself of her goal, to keep herself in among the shadows, to not make waves of any kind, she bowed her head just as they did. And she felt herself, soon, becoming lost in the warbling tone of the chants.

After about a minute or so of this chanting, the collected figures all straightened up, and turned their attention back to the stage.

Syre, too, stared back at the stage.

The speaker cast his—her?—glare over all of them and then declared the meeting over; and wished all present a safe and secure journey back home.

Syre couldn't help but feel slightly let down by her little foray.

She had snuck out of the Palace in search of adventure, in search of intrigue, and she'd found herself in the midst of some secretive—*but not all that interesting*—society.

With the others, she waddled her way toward the exit of the back room, already thinking about how she was going to have to run the gauntlet with Tineoots; that, as if he'd been her father, she would need to explain to him precisely where she had been . . . if he didn't know already. Because, from what Syre had gathered in her time at the Palace, the Council of Ilsnare had a well-developed and intricate network of spies throughout the city; one which had been put in place for decades before Syre first set foot in Ilsnare.

It was known as the Eye.

And she was certain that one spy—at the very least—was dedicated to tracking her footsteps at all times; day or night.

When she had first overheard chatter of the Eye, Syre had become paranoid.

Many times, in the middle of the night, she had woken to scour her quarters for any sign of observers; but had never found anyone.

Later—*now*—she found the existence more of a nuisance than anything malevolent. She had to take care whenever she snuck out of the Palace to ensure that nobody was trailing her. She had taken care tonight. Whether or not she had been followed—whether or not she had been successful in shaking off a follower—she really had no idea.

As Syre found herself in the doorway to the back room, ready to tread on out with the rest of the assembled people, she felt a sharp tug at her cloak.

Before she could even think about resisting, she was yanked aside, out of the assembled group. She found herself, once more, with a dagger pressing into her stomach.

Then a husky whisper.

"You so much as flinch and I'll stick you through, stranger."

POLITE ENQUIRIES

S yre continued to feel the dagger sticking her in the belly as she watched the cloaked figures pass her by. Her heart thumped on hard as she felt the draught from the opened door, out in the side alley she had come through, drift about the back corridors of the pub.

Once the last cloaked figure had left the room behind, the dagger owner stuck her harder still in the stomach. "This way, stranger," he said, guiding her in the direction of the stage; where the speaker and his/her four companions continued to lurk.

Already, Syre felt a chilly sensation drifting down over her. She knew that it was more than just the draught now, that it was brought on from the ice in her blood, and that her magic was warning her of the danger up ahead.

She had no choice, though, not unless . . .

"Brotsboore!" the dagger owner called out.

The cloaked figure who'd addressed the room stirred, then looked over in the dagger owner's direction.

For a long while, the cloaked figure appeared to drink in Syre's appearance—his gaze seemed to almost freeze the blood in her veins; and Syre wondered if she couldn't feel magic in the air . . . she was quite sure she could. She had become quite attuned to her magic. She practised whenever she had a spare moment to do so, and she had become adept at sensing when magic lingered nearby.

And she could sense it here.

The cloaked figures spoke among themselves in a language which Syre didn't understand, and then, apparently some order having been given—or some mutual, group understanding having been agreed—the hoods all drifted down from the heads.

And the dagger was removed from Syre's stomach.

Her own hood was pulled down too.

At first it was overwhelming.

Syre simply couldn't process the sight.

All six of the figures who remained in the back room of *The Soore Whip* had removed the hoods of their cloaks to reveal themselves.

Creatures.

All of them.

First of all, Syre took in the dagger owner, the one who had allowed her entrance, and then denied her exit. To begin with, she couldn't quite believe what she saw. Couldn't quite take in that single eyeball which occupied the middle of his face.

A Cyclops.

The dagger owner; the Cyclops, stared back at her, unblinking, apparently waiting for her to deliver some verdict on him.

Then she turned her attention to look at the speaker for the night's meeting; Brotsboore.

Horned, rash-red skin.

A bald, scabby scalp.

The long, lizard-like snout.

And *black* eyes.

Even through the cloak which Brotsboore wore, Syre could tell that he had pointed shoulders, ones which stuck up against the material like off-cuts of human bone.

Brotsboore stared long and hard at Syre, then smiled, and said, "Syre Dorf." He—because Syre was sure that he could be nothing else—gave a mock curtsey. "We are *charmed* to make your acquaintance, Your Majesty."

Although there should've been about a million other things on Syre's mind right at that second, all she could think to say was, "It's just *Syre* . . . I don't have any royal blood."

Brotsboore's eyes widened at this admission, and then he turned back to survey the four behind him. They were equal to him, if slightly stockier, not as gaunt, and weathered as their leader. Once they had each fed Brotsboore a wicked smile, Brotsboore turned his attention back onto Syre. "Might I ask what brings the Princess of Shellacnass to our humble meeting?"

"I'm not a princess," Syre replied, tasting the bile in her words, and feeling—even to herself—as if she was some kind of petulant toddler.

"Still," Brotsboore continued, "if it's all the same to you, I would quite like to know the reason for your presence here among us this evening."

Syre felt as if thoughts were weaving through her mind.

Her heart leaped up to her throat, but she swallowed it back down.

Determined not to be intimidated by these *Creatures*.

"I . . . I was just curious," Syre said, "that's all—I heard about the meeting . . ."

"*Where?*" Brotsboore put in, his expression suddenly switching from being jovial to being *quite* serious.

Syre thought for a few seconds, about the wise woman she had overheard at the marketplace. And how she had had doughy cheeks, a merry smile; she might've been somebody's grandmother for all Syre knew, and she had *certainly* never done anything to hurt anybody.

From how these creatures were acting, Syre was convinced that they wished nothing but pain and suffering onto somebody who had given away their secret meeting.

"At a marketplace," Syre replied, and then added, "I overheard someone."

"*Who?*" Brotsboore said, carefully treading down the steps which led up to the stage—coming closer to her.

As Brotsboore got closer still, Syre caught the heady, rancid stench of sulphur; a smell like rotten eggs. It sent nausea swirling down to the pit of her stomach. She sunk her teeth down into her lower lip, hoping to mitigate the feeling.

It only half worked.

"I . . . *don't know*," Syre replied finally, "I didn't get a look at them."

For a moment, Syre was certain that Brotsboore would continue his advancement toward her, that he wouldn't be satisfied until he stood with the tip of his nose pressed right up against her own.

Until she felt his horned skin.

But he stopped where he was.

Leaving four or five paces between the two of them.

Brotsboore cocked his head to one side. "Were you followed?" he said, his voice calmer now, more collected.

"No," Syre said, with a shake of her head, glancing back at the Cyclops on her heels. "I don't think so—"

" 'Don't think so', or *weren't?*" Brotsboore shot back at her.

Feeling desperate to get away now, Syre replied, "I *wasn't.*"

"Good," Brotsboore replied, his tone again calming in a fraction of a second. He stared at her long and hard, and Syre got the feeling that he was wondering just how exactly he should punish her—make it so that she never said *anything* about this to anyone . . . but then, when he finally did speak, it was as he turned his back on her, as he padded back up the stage to join with the others; the ones like him. "You may leave," he said.

Before Syre could think of muttering anything by way of reply, she felt the Cyclops's sure hold on her arm return; and she felt herself being yanked clear of the back room of the pub. It wasn't until she was at the door which led out into the side alley that the Cyclops spoke to her. "You're a lucky gal, Syre."

"Really?" Syre said, again trying to keep the blood pumping to her temples out of her voice. "And why's *that?*"

"Anybody else, any other Mortal that Brotsboore had caught there, and they woulda been killed."

Somehow, as Syre felt the door slam shut behind her, as she felt the nibble of the night air at her skin once more, she couldn't help thinking that the Cyclops had been telling the truth.

She could see no reason why he would lie.

BROTHERS

S heilds sat at the wooden table of the kitchen, of the house, where he had grown up. He listened to the yearning silence. It swamped the twisted, cobbled streets outside, and almost seemed to press its meek face up against the glass of the windows, peering in on the warm interior, as if it might be invited in.

Sheilds propped his elbows on the bare wood of the table and picked at the cold leg of lamb which his brother had served him. His brother's wife had prepared it for dinner a little earlier, well before Sheilds had arrived, but, to Sheilds, who had subsisted on nothing more substantial than scraps for the past few weeks—on his journey back to Ilsnare—it was a real feast.

At first, the seasoned meat was almost too much for his taste buds to handle. Whenever he bit into the cold meat, he felt an unpleasant tingling sensation on his tongue; and it was only after he'd taken several bites that he grew accustomed to the feeling.

From the flickering flame of the candle sitting in the middle of the table, just about strong enough to send the shadows scurrying for the corners, he was aware of his brother—Jhang—standing in the doorway.

Staring at him.

Sheilds turned to look at him, took in his ragged, lanky brown hair which seemed to have been smothered in grease. And then he took in his brother's blotchy, pock-marked skin. He was a fabric merchant by trade and, by necessity, had spent a great deal of his time indoors, seeing to the creation of his materials—or else in stomping about the service quarters of castles, offering his wares to the handmaids.

If it hadn't been for his brother's round belly, and his quickly enlarging jowls, Sheilds wasn't certain that anybody would've been able to tell which one of them had spent the past couple of decades in Onderswort.

Both of them seemed to have been knocked about by the world.

"You know," Sheilds said, "it's rather off putting having you stand there, watching me eat." Sheilds gestured across the table, to the bare wooden chair opposite. "Won't you at least sit down." Sheilds turned his attention back to the cold lamb, and then uttered beneath his breath as he took another bite, "Have a drink if you must."

Jhang continued to stand where he was, apparently unwilling to be shifted.

Sheilds took exception at this discourtesy. He allowed the cold leg of lamb to slip down onto the table top, where it landed with a thud. He threw his arms up, beamed a smile at Jhang, then said, "Please, brother, won't you sit? Stop lurking about there as if, at any second, I might shank you in the stomach." Sheilds raised a slight chuckle, then turned his attention back to his leg of lamb. "I'm not in Onderswort any longer, brother—they're not the rules I live by anymore."

Even as Sheilds said it, he thought about all the men—*and women*—he had killed on his way here, on his way to the Crystal City.

There'd been more than a dozen at last count.

Not that it swelled Sheilds with any sense of profound pride.

It was just a fact.

Who he was.

Finally, Jhang acquiesced, he shifted away, out of the doorway, and trudged over to the chair at the opposite side of the table. He hovered over the chair for a couple of seconds before finally perching on the edge of the seat. Apparently not knowing what to do with his hands, he clasped them together tightly in his lap.

Sheilds gave him a slight smirk, a shake of his head and then slipped another piece of cold lamb's flesh in through his lips. "Better," he said, as he chewed.

A draught blew in about the floor of the kitchen and Sheilds felt that old familiar enemy—*cold*—bring his skin out in goose pimples. The draught sent the candle flame flickering, almost extinguishing it, plunging the room into darkness for several seconds before the flame rose up anew.

Sheilds nodded over Jhang's shoulder, to the fireplace on the other side of the kitchen. "You wouldn't spark up a little kindling, would you?" Sheilds said. "It's just that I've grown so weary of the cold—I don't think that I could stand so much as a single second more of it."

Jhang didn't reply, staring down at his hands clasped in his lap. When he spoke, his tone remained a mumble, almost unable to be heard. "Ain't no kindling," he said.

"Hmm?" Sheilds said, picking at the last of the flesh attached to the leg of lamb. "I'm afraid you'll have to speak up if I'm to hear you."

This time Jhang glanced up, and met Sheilds's eye. "There ain't no kindling to be had." Jhang gave a shake of his head. "Worth more than its weight in gold these days. The Council hands out any of the surplus to the poor in the Burrows so that *they* have some warmth."

Sheilds furrowed his brow. " 'The Council', just what on *Earth* is that?"

Jhang gave a shrug, then met his brother's eye for a fraction of a second. "It's what happened after the Magical Siege, after Louson Dorf took the Palace." He shrugged again then rolled his eyes. "He didn't want the power he took"—here Jhang gave a weak, wary smile—"call him the *Hitchking* . . . like he went and 'hitched' the throne then left it behind." Jhang shook his head. "Anyway, Louson Dorf assigned it to a Council of Wisemen, just like they do in the magical world."

Here Jhang hocked up a wad of phlegm and spat it out at his feet.

Sheilds felt a little of the phlegm splatter against his trouser leg. For an infraction such as this, Sheilds might've found reason to *kill* . . . but a stranger was one thing, and his brother another.

Jhang continued, "They're the ones with the big ideas—ones that're bringing Ilsnare to its knees faster than you can say."

Sheilds chewed up the last of his lamb and then, spying the pile of discarded bones off in the corner of the kitchen, he tossed it over there. It landed with a distant, muted *thud.*

When Sheilds looked over the table, to his brother on the other side, he realised that Jhang was staring right back at him.

"You can't stay here, you know," Jhang said. "The wife won't have it—won't *allow* it."

Sheilds felt his chest tighten. He had expected something like this. Some sort of *resistance.* He had had a great deal of time to think about how he might respond to it, and he stuck to that plan now.

Sheilds crossed his arms over his chest, eyed Jhang for a long few moments. "I'd like you to help me find a job," he said. "Do you think you'd at least be able to do that?"

Jhang stayed very still for several moments before finally breaking free. He met Sheilds's eye, and gave him a decisive nod.

ILSNARE PALACE

When Syre pressed herself up against the stone wall of Ilsnare Palace, arriving to the eastern wall, she could hear her heart beating hard in her eardrums. It had been a close call, back there, at *The Soore Whip.* She could quite easily have got her throat slit.

So, why was it that she could hardly stop herself grinning from ear to ear?

Her breathing came shallow and it took a great deal of strength simply to remember to draw the air into her lungs, and then to exhale.

All over her skin, she felt a prickling sensation; the ice magic which flowed through her veins.

She glanced up to the ramparts above her. She spotted motion there. A Royal Guard.

She knew enough about sneaking out afterhours that the guards would let fly with their crossbow bolts and ask questions later . . . if the matter of her death at the hands of Royal Guards made it as far as the Council then she was certain the Wisemen would absolve the guard of any responsibility.

He would only have been following orders.

She would be the one in the wrong.

She waited a couple of heartbeats, and then, pressing her body up even harder against the Palace wall, she closed her eyes. She murmured incantations to herself—one of the ones she had learned so long ago, as a mere child, from one of her mother's books.

It was a gradual sensation; like the stirring of ice magic within her blood.

Slowly but surely, she felt an oddly freeing sensation; as if her skin was being painlessly separated from her bones. As if she was leaving some great weight behind.

She rose up and out of herself.

Her arms had now taken the form of wings.

Tiny wings.

Bird wings.

A *crow's* wings.

She looked down on her body below, frozen, up against the wall.

It had taken her so long to reach this level of control, to be able to practise such a subtle level of magic.

She fluttered up to the ramparts and then extended her talons, readied to land upon the stone.

When she did land there, she could see out across the whole of the ramparts, to the Royal Guards as they patrolled their ground; swords sheathed in their hilts.

She settled there, on the stone, for several seconds before rising again.

She felt the chilly air swilling about the ramparts, blowing around her tiny bird's body—her *crow's* body—but she maintained her force to launch herself upward once more.

As she soared up higher and higher, she found that she could make out the whole of Ilsnare, the scattering of torches illuminating the labyrinthine side streets. A little way further off, across the city, she made out the River Ils; its surface grim and grey, glistening in the little moonlight which made it through the overcast skies.

It was never-stopping.

Seemingly never-ending.

Syre often fantasised about following its curves out across the plain lands of Shellacnass, of arriving all the way out to the sea, where nobody would know her.

Nobody would know her as Syre Dorf, 'Princess of Shellacnass'.

She would be able to start again.

Didn't everyone deserve a fresh beginning?

She lingered in the air, feeling the swill of the warmth from the rising thermals beneath her wings. And she thought long and hard about just fluttering her wings, leaving her mortal body behind; and following the river out to sea.

But there was still a doubt lodged in her mind.

That she wasn't strong enough.

That she wouldn't be able to control her magic.

And that she would find trouble.

No matter what she did.

As this realisation dawned on Syre, she felt her crow's body sinking in the air, drifting down—*gently*—to the ground; back to her mortal body.

When she felt herself return to her body, there was a sudden *jerk*, as if her brain was getting used to the idea that her spirit might come and go as it pleased.

She straightened up, felt drained by her efforts; but, at the same time, deeply fulfilled. There was almost nothing else Syre loved more in this world than putting her magic to use.

And, what was more, she now knew all the guards' movements. And how to sneak her way into the Palace.

A SLEEPWALKER RETURNS

S yre felt the warmth as she trod along the corridor which led to her quarters.

That was one of the nice things about having House Staff, that they dedicated a twenty-four-hour blazing fire entirely to Syre; as if they were paralytically afraid that Syre might sleepwalk in the middle of the night and end up somewhere along the corridor, catching a chill.

If only they knew the truth, about where Syre had been that evening.

Then they might turn their attentions to other matters.

To the more tangible dangers.

Feeling her stomach quivering with hunger pangs, Syre thought about heading down to the kitchens and getting a midnight snack. A member of the staff would be sleeping on some straw on the floor of the kitchen, ready to cook up anything a member of the household might request at a moment's notice.

But Syre was wary of stirring their sleep.

Of violating their comfort; not even considering her own interests in having her night-time activities go undiscovered.

So Syre consigned herself to having to wait for breakfast and trod along the corridor, toward her quarters.

She had hardly reached the door when she caught the impression that somebody was trailing her heels. She glanced back. Looked into the shadows.

Her heart fluttered up into her throat.

Her blood ran cold.

And her veins itched with ice magic.

After her transformation into a crow, outside the Palace walls, she wasn't certain that she retained the strength to summon so much as a simple enchantment to protect herself.

But—*if threatened*—she would try.

"I can see you there," Syre managed to get out, her voice staying surprisingly even and authoritative. She supposed that, somehow, the princess syndrome which she found herself battling against daily had got into her brain on a subconscious level.

She had a—perhaps ill-placed—sense of ownership and protection for Ilsnare Palace.

In reality, though, Syre could see nothing in the shadows. Only shapes. There might be anybody—any*thing*—or nothing there . . . but if there was nothing or nobody there then she had no fear of looking ridiculous.

She reached down to the waist of her brother Lou's sheepskin cloak before realising that she hadn't brought along so much as a dagger on her night-time venture. She believed in the old woman's adage of 'a knife bringing only trouble', no matter in whose possession it rested.

She preferred for her enemies to think her weak, and so to *underestimate* her . . . so that they'd never see the hex which would knock them onto their back.

Open up a hole in their chest.

Syre stared off into the shadows for another few seconds before realising that there *wasn't* anybody there after all.

Feeling her breath coming more easily now, she turned her attention back to the corridor ahead.

Already, the soft, silk sheets of her bed, and the embering fireplace emanating warmth all around the room seemed an impossibly relaxing dream.

A dream she was about to make real.

As she trod on her way, she rolled her neck, feeling the muscles *click* and *groan* in protest. If Tineoots had been there, he would've scolded her for such an *unladylike* gesture.

But he wasn't there, she was all alone.

When Syre got into her bedroom, it was just as wonderful as she'd imagined.

The coal fire crackled away in the corner, sending wave upon wave of warmth through the room.

She shrugged off the sheepskin coat, draped it over the back of one of the oak chairs standing at the dressing table. She undressed herself and then slipped beneath the sheets of her four-poster bed. Although there were netted curtains, she never liked to draw them. It made her feel claustrophobic to shut the rest of the world out, to confine herself in such a small space . . . as if she might trap herself.

It was with that thought, the thought that danger might be lurking all around, that Syre felt herself drifting away; losing herself to unconsciousness.

And to sleep.

But, just as she felt herself on the threshold of dreams, she heard a thick, familiar voice.

"Naughty, naughty. 'A secret kept is a burden taken'."

MIDNIGHT MEETING

S yre blinked back the darkness which surrounded her. All that illuminated the room was the gentle, orange light from the coal fire. And that was only enough to outline shadows. Shapes.

The glass double doors which opened out onto the balcony, which—itself—offered an unrivalled view out over the Palace grounds and the Crystal City beyond.

Syre could feel her heart beating hard in her chest. She glanced about her, determined to see him—to at least *know* where he was.

Where Flucknor was.

Failing to locate him, Syre gave up, and spoke into the darkness.

" 'A secret kept is a burden taken', " she repeated, "is that something they taught you at the monastery, at Ravensbark? Back when you were a monk?"

Her words returned to her from the darkness, unanswered.

She kept her eyes peeled for any sign of moving shadows, but could see nothing at all.

If only she hadn't exerted herself with her magic outside the Palace walls then she might have the strength to summon an illumination charm . . . but, if she was determined about anything at all, it was *not* to show weakness in Flucknor's presence.

Although Flucknor had come to stay with them as a novice—*apprentice*—monk, he had become, under Lou's care, quite a fine ice mage in his own right.

Or so Syre believed . . . because that *had* to be what he and Lou spent all their time alone discussing, hadn't it?

All that she had over him—all that she *felt* she had over him—was the mystery of her dark magic; a magic which Flucknor was determined to remain ignorant of; let alone practise. The two of them might well have ice magic flowing in their veins, but they were worlds apart in terms of the Lightness and Darkness which divided them.

"All right," Syre said, with a slight sigh, "I give up—where *are* you?"

But it felt as if she was still speaking into the darkness, as if Flucknor's voice had only sounded within the confines of her own skull. And she was certain that this was Flucknor's desired effect . . . that he wanted to have the upper hand in this particular midnight meeting.

Finally, Syre felt the mattress sink to her left. Her heart skipped a beat. She turned to look.

There he was.

Sitting on the edge of the bed.

She took in his form in the nearly depleted light. She thought about how she had been only eleven, twelve summers old when she had first met him. A decade ago now. She recalled his fragile nose, and delicate chin. How he had been lanky, almost without a single muscle on his body.

But those features were gone now.

Five summers her senior, he had fleshed out into a full-grown man.

While Syre was now twenty-one summers old; Flucknor was twenty-six.

Twenty-*seven* soon.

However, he still possessed those ice-blue eyes, and his shoulder-length, silver-blond hair.

Almost as if the boy he had once been was peering out from within.

Before Syre could say anything further Flucknor leaned forward and planted an intense, soft kiss on her lips. For a long time, Syre felt all the thoughts leak free from her mind, and she found herself relaxing—*truly relaxing*—for the first time that evening.

She could feel his heart beating through his lips.

She could breathe in the thick, soapy smell that seemed to linger about him. Some of the habits of the monastery—of Ravensbark— he hadn't been able to shake; such as the one which compelled monks to bathe every morning and every night in order to preserve the sanctity of the monastery.

When Flucknor broke off the kiss, he retreated from her, to the edge of the bed.

His lips were pressed tightly together as he sat, staring at her from out of the darkness. "You were out there tonight, in the street," he said.

Syre felt her body lock up tight. She stared harder at him through the gloom. Finally, though, she got a hold on herself.

Why in the world did she *care* what Flucknor thought of her?

"So what?" she shot back, surprised at her frank, slightly combative tone.

"It's dangerous," Flucknor replied, looking away from her now, fiddling with his index finger.

"Why?" Syre replied.

Flucknor didn't say anything to that.

He was the only one who knew that Syre had continued her studies, that Syre had continued to pursue her dark magic. And it also followed that he knew well just how she would be able to defend herself if she came across trouble.

Like she had tonight.

It was then that Syre told herself that, if she'd wanted to—if she'd *really* wanted—she could easily have defended herself against those . . . those *Creatures.*

As Syre allowed the implication of what Flucknor was saying to hit her deeper, she felt anger flare up within her chest. "You met with the Eye tonight—didn't you?"

Flucknor shook his head. "No," he said, and then a slight smile appeared on his lips. "And I don't think I'd know where to start looking for them, let alone pumping them for information."

That was one of the mysteries of the Eye which often bothered Syre, how even she—*a de facto princess*—had no idea just who might be involved in the network of spies. And even if a spy was asked directly, it was understood that they would lie. She supposed that was for the safety of the city, and the Kingdom. So that, if she was captured, she wouldn't so much as be able to point the finger to any member of the Eye.

Because, she knew, so many citizens of Ilsnare would *kill* to find out who it was spying on their daily routines; who was responsible for the 'anonymous' tips which led to arrests for counterfeiting or contra-banding citywide.

Syre, herself, hadn't quite ever seen the issue with this level of surveillance, as long as it helped to keep the citizens of Ilsnare honest . . . but, to be fair, she really hadn't given the matter a lot of thought.

When she had decided, years before, that being a princess was the very last thing on her mind, she had done so with the reasoning that it wasn't only the pomp of being a princess which bored her, but all the governance which was to come.

And the Eye was another one of these *matters of governance.*

She had to admit, though, that not knowing who was a member of the Eye lent itself to the idea that she *always* had to be on her best behaviour . . . that she never quite knew who might be watching her from the shadows.

Whenever she thought to remember.

There was a long silence in Syre's quarters as the two of them processed what Flucknor had just said. In the end, Syre was the one to break the silence. "So," she said, "you *followed* me, then?"

Flucknor gave her a nod, and then the hint of another grin. "That was some job you did on your transformation—you've been practising, I can tell."

"Hmm," Syre replied, and then, wanting to change the subject—finding her magical development a somewhat *personal* matter—she added, "Did you see what happened in the pub—in *The Soore Whip?*"

Flucknor shook his head. "No," he said, "I waited outside, in the alleyway."

Syre silently scolded herself for not having noticed.

For not having spent more time *looking.*

"What did happen?" Flucknor said.

Although he asked the question casually, with a light tone, Syre could tell that he was pressing her, that he wanted to get an answer out of her—if not to pass onto her brother; then for his own understanding of the situation.

Syre made her choice.

"Oh," she said, "nothing—just the usual: ale, brandy wine, you know?"

Flucknor continued to stare at her closely. "Why'd you go in through the back-alley entrance?"

Syre was surprised by her quick thinking; the words seemed to tumble out of her mouth before she'd even had a chance to fully consider them. "Do you think I'd get *any* peace at all walking in through the front door of an establishment like that?" She smirked back at him. "I've got my own little room around the back, and an arrangement with the proprietor."

Flucknor's eyes remained glued to hers, then he said, "I've never seen you going there before."

Syre arched her eyebrows. "You mean that you've *followed* me before?"

At this, even in the darkness, Syre could tell that Flucknor blushed slightly.

There was that young boy again . . . nothing more than a teenage monk finding his place in the world. She was glad that he wasn't a monk any longer.

On impulse, Syre reached out and grasped hold of his hand in hers. She looked deeply into his eyes, then said, "You'll stay with me tonight?"

Flucknor squeezed her hand back, then glanced over his shoulder as if somebody might be watching on from the doorway.

Of course there was nobody there.

He turned back to her, gave her hand a final squeeze then rose to his feet. "No," he said, "I promised your brother that I'd see to a matter before morning—before *breakfast.*"

"And that 'matter' wasn't keeping an eye on me?"

"No," Flucknor replied.

"Then what?" Syre said.

Flucknor said nothing. He took a couple of steps backward, in the direction of the door to her chamber. "I . . . really can't say . . ."

Syre glared back at him. Again, she felt as though her lips were miles ahead of her conscious thoughts. "The Webbing Armoury, isn't it?" she said. "You're going to check up on the Blade, Bow and Cloak?"

The Webbing Blade, Bow and Cloak were nothing short of the most powerful magical artefacts in the whole of Shellacnass; and, for an ice mage, they represented the mightiest of tools to complete whatever they yearned for.

But, mostly, an unmatched ability for destruction.

Again, though, Flucknor said nothing at all. He only continued his retreat, to the door of Syre's bedroom. When he reached the doorway itself, he lingered, as if waiting for some inevitable question.

Syre decided to play her part. "It's okay," she said, "I know you can't tell me where the Webbing Armoury is located—I know that neither you or my brother trust me."

Flucknor remained in the doorway, as if he was waiting to be dismissed.

Syre often wondered if this deferential nature of his was some sort of a hangover from his life among the monks. Despite his relatively swift progress into becoming a mage, he always seemed to be awaiting an order of some sort.

She reached up to her forehead and fed him a mock salute; the gesture of her fingers to the temple, the gesture which the Royal Guards used to greet one another.

Seeming to catch this subtlety, Flucknor mumbled a goodnight, and slipped out of her quarters.

Only once Syre heard his footsteps disappear off down the corridor did she allow herself to tumble back into the impossibly soft pillows of her bed.

Here, in Ilsnare Palace, she had never felt so out of place in all her life.

GOOD, HONEST WORK

When his brother **Jhang** had claimed that his wife wouldn't like Sheilds's presence in the house, he hadn't been lying.

Sheilds thought about the uncomfortable silence at breakfast, at the surprise which'd quickly sketched Jhang's wife's face only to be replaced by an uncomfortably polite expression. How she'd served him his runny eggs, and given him a pair of loaves, warm out of the oven, with a sour expression she'd believed he hadn't noticed.

Sheilds had killed women for fewer discourtesies.

But she was his brother's wife, and her death would've been so pointless, so at odds with the reason why Sheilds had returned to Ilsnare:

To start again.

To go straight.

Good, honest work.

Since Sheilds had nothing except for the weeks-old, once-white undershirt he'd worn on his journey to Ilsnare, Jhang kindly offered him several items of clothing from out of his own wardrobe.

In the end, Sheilds was relatively pleased with the crimson tunic and beige pair of work trousers his brother saw fit to provide him with. And he could tell from Jhang's wife's expression, as the two of them went out the door, that she was less than put-out by the fact that Jhang was ridding himself of these particular clothes.

The two of them strolled through the cobbled streets of Ilsnare; alive with motion and colour now, almost *too* vibrant for Sheilds to understand.

On his way here, he had had—almost by force of necessity—to avoid built-up settlements for fear of being recognised as an outsider . . . for being correctly tagged as a murderer.

And there always was a victim.

"Just up here," Jhang said, his voice just about trailing out from the corner of his mouth.

They turned onto the Crystal Causeway, the road which led along the bank of the River Ils, and which presented the pathway to Ilsnare Palace.

Sheilds took in the market stalls, selling all manner of goods. Berries, fruits, vegetables that he hadn't seen in years, not since he was a child in Ilsnare; before he was sent away to Onderswort.

The air was all at once sweet and full of *goodness.*

He listened to the patter of the merchants as they barked out after Sheilds and his brother, imploring them to buy from them.

As Sheilds trod on further, he felt an almost irrepressible hunger rising in his stomach. And he couldn't help but think back to the wonderful, *sloppy* eggs and bread Jhang's wife had served him that morning at breakfast.

What most attracted Sheilds's attention at the market stalls, though, were the weapons.

The daggers, the swords, the sabres. Their blades all shimmering in the morning sun, sending blinding golden rays right back into Sheilds's eyes.

A couple of times, he found the daylight so bright that he had to hold his forearm up to shield himself from the glare.

He was a man who was used to back alleys and night-time shadows.

It wasn't often he walked down a main market street in broad daylight.

Finally, after leading him down a series of switchback alleys, Jhang came to a halt outside a ragged, wooden door. Sheilds saw that the door no longer fit its doorway—if it ever had. Jhang bashed his fist on the door several times and then glanced around, as if somebody might be watching from the shadows.

There was a scrum of activity behind the door before it opened.

Standing in the doorway, much to Sheilds's surprise, was a woman of about twenty summers.

When he had first looked upon her, though, he had taken her for an elderly woman. He realised that her hair had prematurely turned grey.

But it was her soft, wrinkle-free skin which illustrated her youth.

The woman wore a neat, light-purple robe, with the rope about the waist drawn in tightly. She examined the two of them standing in the doorway with a bored look, while chewing on something.

Sheilds speculated that the woman might be attractive if she took better care of herself . . . if she thought to smile once in a while.

"What is it?" the woman said, and then thrust her tongue into the side of her cheek.

All of a sudden Jhang seemed to become a little fidgety, and Sheilds wondered just how much of a 'sure thing' this gainful employment might be.

"Thought you could do with some muscle," Jhang got out.

The woman screwed up her eyes. "You?" she said, almost spitting the word.

"No," Jhang said, his cheeks flushing slightly before slipping Sheilds a sidelong glance. "My brother."

The woman turned her attention to Sheilds, and Shields did his best to smile back, although he knew—even when he *tried*—his smile resembled more of a grimace.

The woman's expression didn't alter notably when she switched back to looking at Jhang. She shook her head. "Nah," she said, "Not looking for any sort of trouble here."

When she made to shut the door in their faces, Jhang acted quickly—much more quickly than Sheilds might've *expected* a big man like him to act. Jhang jammed his arm up against the back of the door, stopping her from closing it.

The woman struggled a couple of times, shoving her shoulder against the other side of the door, trying desperately to get it to close.

Jhang shifted a glance back to Sheilds, and gave him a *wicked* smile which Sheilds himself might well have been proud of . . . perhaps there was more to his brother than an untamed wife.

Jhang turned his attention back to the woman, who had allowed the door to open wide again, and was standing there, her arms crossed over her chest.

"Whatcha want?" she said, her voice bolshie, but defeated.

Jhang spoke clearly, in a vaguely threatening way which—Sheilds was sure—was extremely effective when dealing with petulant handmaidens who 'weren't *that* interested' in the materials he had to sell. "I want you to give my brother here a job."

The woman cast a glance over Sheilds once more, her mind clearly unchanged, but at least now receptive to persuasion.

"From what I can tell," Jhang said, "you don't have any sort of adequate protection here . . . at least"—Jhang glanced past her, into the darkened interior—"I don't see anybody coming running." He shifted his attention back to her. "Or are they all asleep?"

The woman didn't reply.

And Sheilds could tell that he had her.

"Now," Jhang continued, "what I'm gonna suggest is that you take on my brother here, or else you might find yourself in something of a sticky situation one of these nights"—he bust out in a grin—"and that'd be awfully unfortunate for your business."

The woman said nothing.

She stood still in the doorway.

When she turned her eyes onto Sheilds, her mouth twisted about the corners, and then she said, "Come on up—you'll be wanting lodging too, I suspect?"

With that, the woman disappeared into the building, leaving the door open, and—apparently—expecting Sheilds to follow.

Sheilds dithered in the back alley for a couple of moments before turning to Jhang. "You know," he said, "you've got something of the devil's touch about you."

Jhang smirked in reply, then reached up and clasped Sheilds's shoulder. He swayed on past him, headed out of the alley, back in the direction they'd come. "You just keep your nose clean, eh, brother? And dontcha come knocking on my door if you get into trouble."

Jhang gave Sheilds no opportunity to reply to this because he slunk off into the shadows of the back alley before he got a chance.

But, anyway, Sheilds had nothing to say to his brother.

He had only respect for him.

Never—not in a million years—had he thought he had it in him.

Sheilds turned his attention back to the doorway ahead.

The door clear.

A new life awaiting.

Full of hope.

BREAKFAST

Syre just lay in bed, feeling the warm sunrays against the backs of her eyelids when she woke the next day. She savoured the moment for several minutes, feeling that vaguely *itchy* sensation as the sun combatted the ice magic within her veins.

Like her brother—like *all* those who had ice magic running through their blood—her time was the night . . . and her strength was the moon. But that didn't mean that she refused to walk in weakness; to meet the day and all its threat *head on* . . . not to do so meant giving the magic the opportunity to consume her whole, and she had no intention of allowing that to happen.

She had so many more adventures to live.

So much to *explore.*

As Syre rose up out of bed, still dressed in the underclothes she had worn out in the street the night before, she caught the scent of butter carrying on the air. When she turned her attention to the doorway of her quarters, she half expected to see Flucknor standing in the gap, some sort of knowing glance on his face.

Some *superior* expression lining his eyes.

And then he would kiss her again.

But there was no sign of Flucknor this morning, and, to be honest, after his admission that he had followed her the night before, she was quite glad.

Sometimes she liked to be left alone.

Left to her own devices.

Syre padded off into her washroom, to the stone basin she had there. A bucket of water stood to the side—water which had, *once upon a time*, been warm, but which was now freezing cold.

Still, Syre enjoyed the sensation of thrusting her wrists into the bucket and feeling the chilly water soothe her skin as if she'd been afflicted by sunburn.

She washed herself quickly and dressed in a light-green robe, one which matched the colour of her eyes most days; her eyes seemed to almost have a mind of their own, shifting from blue to green, and back again, at will.

When she'd been a little girl, Syre had wondered if it hadn't had something to do with her particular mood that day ... and, as she'd got older, she'd become more and more convinced of it.

It was funny to think that most children left their wonder behind with their childhood, while Syre's had only increased hundredfold as she learned more and more about the ice magic which flowed through her blood.

She went down to breakfast in the kitchen bare-footed, and caught a chiding stare off Tineoots for her trouble.

Today he wore the wispy-grey colour of the Crystal City Royal Family ... the same colour which was worn by the Royal Guards, and which, Syre often thought during her night-time excursions, made them look like wandering ghosts.

There was nobody else about the kitchen, and she supposed that the staff had all gone off duty until the evening meal; leaving her breakfast out for her.

"Your Highness?" Tineoots said as Syre passed by.

Syre thought long and hard about settling herself down on the wooden bench before her, to the feast laid out there. But, instead, she turned to look back at him.

"You do realise what time it is?" Tineoots said.

Syre gave a shrug.

"It's *well* after midday," Tineoots replied.

She took in Tineoots's face; the sketched-on wrinkles about his eyes, the way that his small mouth seemed out of proportion with the rest of his features. He had cotton wool-like tufts of curly white hair sprouting in a semi-circle about the crown of his head. She often wondered why men of a certain age didn't simply cut their losses and shave their scalp ... stubble was *far* more attractive than withered, old hair.

Finally, she turned her attention to how Tineoots's fingernails were perfectly manicured ... certainly in far superior condition than her own fingernails might aspire to be.

"And?" Syre shot back.

Tineoots blinked several times, and then, after closing his eyes tight for a couple of seconds, he stared back out at her. "It's *not* becoming," he said, "not of a *queen*."

Syre thought about responding to him, about telling him that she had *no* intention of even being a princess—much less a queen. And, anyway, it wasn't like her brother was at death's door. He wasn't even ill. He was only detached from the real world, shut off in his own quarters.

Finally, Syre took her place at the table, already greedily eyeing the chunk of butter and bread awaiting her. She could see that raisins had been baked into the bread, and cinnamon. It was as if the kitchen staff could read her mind.

Right as she was about to pick up the knife and fork—her *silver* cutlery—Tineoots cleared his throat. "What?" Syre said, glaring in his direction.

Tineoots cocked his head to one side and gave her a sly smile; one of those smiles which told her, instinctively, that Tineoots had some sort of information which he *knew* was going to adversely affect her. "Your brother—the *King*—was down here this morning."

Syre leaned back from the breakfast table, all the delicious-looking fruits—*the bread*—forgotten for a moment. "What?" she said, feeling a numbing cold settle over her. "What'd you mean?"

"Oh," Tineoots said, smiling wider now, clearly delighted to have caught her in a trap. "He was looking for you—hoping to catch you before you headed about your day." Tineoots turned his attention downward, onto those famously manicured fingernails of his. "I had the misfortune of telling him that you hadn't yet *started* your day."

Syre hardly registered this implied slight, her mind was still fixed on the facts.

Her brother.

Lou.

Down here.

About the castle.

Out of his quarters.

She leaped up from the table, stalked across the kitchen, her breakfast now forgotten.

"Your Highness, where are you going?" Tineoots called after her.

But Syre didn't so much as pause to answer him.

THE RECLUSIVE KING

Syre's feet felt lighter with each step as she clambered up the spiral staircase leading to her brother's quarters.

To the Throne Room.

Like always, the large oak doors were kept shut—no trace of light emanating from within. She thought about knocking and then reminded herself that, whenever she had knocked before, Lou hadn't so much as bothered to give her a response.

So, instead, she merely turned the door handle and trod in through the gap.

Crimson velvet hung from the walls and there was a floor of emerald marble beneath Syre's feet . . . not that she could make it out in the gloom.

Up above, the gorgeous, crystal dome which ordinarily showed off either a panorama of the day's sky, or the glittering stars at night, had long ago been covered up with hanging, grey drapes—the same colour as the House Staff's clothes, and the uniforms of the Royal Guards.

Only a little sunlight leaked in about the edges of the material.

She glanced about the Throne Room, to the throne itself; but her brother wasn't there.

She turned her attention to the corner of the room, to the part of the Throne Room which was cordoned off from the rest with another velvet curtain. Peeking up from just above the curtain, she could make out the tips of Lou's own four-poster bed.

She supposed that this was where he was.

Taking care not to make a sound with her footsteps, Syre trod over to the curtain, shifted it back and peered around to the other side.

The bed was empty.

The sheets all made:

Crisp and neat.

The air smelled lightly of lavender, and, from her own run-ins with chambermaids, Syre knew that they were the ones responsible for the scent.

Already, Syre could feel her nose begin to twitch with an allergy, and she backed away from the bed, and back out into the Throne Room.

It was eerie to stand in the Throne Room, with nobody else here. She thought that if she called out, she might hear her own voice reverberate about the corridors of the entire Palace. Sometimes she had the urge to fill her lungs with air and to scream just as *hard* as she could.

To lose control.

But she pressed her lips together.

Made no sound.

She left the Throne Room behind, only to find, lurking outside the doors, Tineoots.

The two of them examined one another, with a sort of mutual loathing, before Tineoots cleared his throat and said, "Your brother is down at the stables."

Syre just nodded in reply, and skittered away from him.

She left Tineoots behind to, no doubt, walk into the Throne Room and stand alone there for himself, left with his thoughts to consider the more *regal* of times; when rich and thick royal blood really did flow within the walls of Ilsnare Palace.

When Syre reached the stables, it was only to see a pair of horses disappear out through the side gates of the Palace, off into the city beyond.

She turned on the stable boy, standing about a little awkwardly, his eyes wide as he stared off after the pair of departing horses. "Saddle one up for me," she said.

And the stable boy did as she instructed.

The stable boy saddled up a horse with a pale, blue-grey hide; a tone which, Syre was certain, had been selected with meticulous care so as to match the Royal Colours of Ilsnare Palace.

She watched on as the horse's exhalations formed stream from its mouth and nostrils.

Syre had always had something of an affinity for horses, and over the years she'd spent at the Palace, with *nothing else to do* besides listen to visiting tutors drone on about this and that, she'd dedicated herself to practising horse-riding.

Often, and much to Tineoots's disappointment, unchaperoned, she would saddle up a horse and ride out of the Palace, then out onto the plains. She would ride for hours and hours, seeing how far she could get away from the pit-black walls of Ilsnare.

See how far she would dare to venture from the place she termed, for want of a better word, her home.

Today, though, she wasn't going to indulge such childish whims.

Today was an adventure of a different sort.

Today was a matter of pursuit.

From the stables, she sourced a travelling cloak and threw it on over her light green robe; a piece of clothing which was far more apt for lounging about at court than gallivanting on horseback.

Negating the ladies' step which the stable boy had provided, Syre grasped tight to the reins and then hauled herself up onto the horse's back.

As Syre squeezed the horse with her thighs, out through the gates of the Palace, and into the city beyond, she breathed in the thick, musky, familiar scent of horse hide. She caught the dry taste at the back of her mouth. She felt the warmth from the horse's body passing through her skin, mitigating the winter's chill. Her heartbeats seemed almost to synchronise with the gentle *clip-clop* of the horse's hoofs against cobblestones.

And her whole body relaxed—the opposite of the tightening of *everything* which seemed to happen to most other human beings when they mounted a horse.

She often wondered why this was, if it was because of her magic, because she knew that, if the worst came to the worst, she could cast a healing charm, fix up a broken arm, or a gashed leg.

In the end, though, she settled for the idea that there seemed nothing more natural than to be seated up on a horse's back, escaping from something as fast as possible.

Up ahead, Syre caught sight of the pair of horses.

She saw, sure enough, her brother seated upon one.

And, on the other, Flucknor.

She felt her whole body become caught with a tremor ... because she was certain of just what this meant. Of just why her brother Lou and Flucknor were together, out in the city.

She had only to think of what Flucknor had said the night before. They were headed for the Webbing Armoury.

THE WEBBING ARMOURY

S yre felt her whole body seize up with tension. Her horse seemed to register the change in her because it attempted to head off in a different direction entirely, away from the trail they were pursuing.

Syre gripped the reins tightly in her fists and steered the horse back after Lou and Flucknor, determined to stay on their trail.

They led the way through winding streets, the twisting, turning passageways which surrounded Ilsnare and which were designed to fool any would-be invaders laying siege to the city, attempting to storm the Palace.

To make things as difficult as possible for them while the archers and crossbowmen rained their projectiles down on them from above, from the notches in the stonework of the houses.

Or else from their stations on the rooftops.

Finally, Lou and Flucknor emerged out onto the main street of Ilsnare: the Crystal Causeway; a beautifully smooth, cobblestone road which ran alongside the River Ils. And which was home to most of the merchants of the city . . . those who, by hook or by crook, managed to nail down one of these choice spots.

Even despite her struggle to keep her eyes on Lou and Flucknor, Syre couldn't help but take in the gorgeous hanging baskets; all of them filled with winter-blooming flowers. The sun had already turned its afternoon golden shade; the shade which told Syre that, soon, night would fall again.

Was that what Lou and Flucknor were hoping for?

The cover of darkness?

Several times, as she urged her horse onward along the cobblestones of the Crystal Causeway, she felt her horse's hoofs slip. When she glanced down, she realised that the cobblestones were still glazed with ice—the ice which glistened and sparkled in the sun, as if the cobblestones consisted of some precious stone.

She looked to the River Ils, and to the boats moored to the banks; and the many merchants and citizens doing business.

When she breathed in now, she smelled the silt and the mud, and the slightly *fishy* stale odour of the river. The cries of the merchants, looking to drum up business, and their clients, bartering them down as low as they dared, filled the air.

In the middle distance, she caught sight of the crystal rooftops of Ilsnare, all of them beginning to catch the dimming sun's rays; setting their glass roofs ablaze with fire.

And, beyond that, Syre could see the hills, growing up out of the plains. Although it was impossible to see with the naked eye, she was certain that she could make out the purply haze of the foothills of the Sable Mountains—of the place which'd been a refuge for her and her people for at least the span of several seasons.

It was strange that a certain sadness lingered whenever she thought of her stay at the encampments, in the foothills of the Sable Mountains. And it saddened her more to think of Sully and Rut, her brother's companions, and the ones who had stood at his side during the raid on Ilsnare, and who had been promoted to generals in the Royal Guards.

Although Sully and Rut were still very much present in the Royal Guards, they were no longer in the city. The Council of Wisemen had seen fit to assign Sully and Rut, each, a role in the Kingdom.

And so Sully had become: Sulliman, Royal Protector of the Plains; while Rut had become: Rutterness, Royal Guardian of the Waterways.

Although these roles were supposed to be promotions of a sort, Syre couldn't help feeling that the Council of Wisemen had contrived to remove such faithful friends of Lou's from the city; and, in so doing, had made sure that Lou had as few personal allies as possible.

Often she wondered if this was the reason at the centre of Lou's reclusion.

He simply didn't trust those around him any longer.

And he wished to get shot of his throne just as badly as Syre wished to leave behind any sort of pretence that she was a 'princess'.

But she hardly spoke with Lou anymore.

For a few moments, Syre lost sight of Lou.

To begin with, she was certain that she had lost him completely. She trotted onward, the people on the Causeway parting to allow her horse through, unwilling to be stomped beneath her horse's hoofs.

She turned around in the saddle, and then spotted the two of them: Lou and Flucknor, heading over one of the single-file, stone bridges which passed over the Ils.

She brought the reins down on her horse's neck with a sharp *snap*, and led it on, after them.

When she got to the other side of the Ils, to the much quieter side street off to the side, she again spotted Flucknor and Lou making their way down a tight passageway.

Her heart bounced up in her throat.

She tore on after them, knocking over an old woman's fruit stand as she did so. As she went, she turned in the saddle and called an apology over her shoulder.

The old woman stood among the scattered fruits with a thunderous expression on her face.

When Syre turned back in the direction her horse travelled, she wondered if the woman would've been so put out if she'd known Syre's identity.

That she was Princess of Shellacnass.

Another strange thing was how the people seemed to adore her—*and her brother*—without them having to do anything at all.

As if their mere existence was enough.

Syre carried on along the tight passageway, ducking several times to avoid the rickety wooden balconies of the upper floors of the houses. And then, as she turned the corner, as she laid eyes on the two she followed, she realised they had dismounted their horses and were now blocking the way forward. She brought her horse to a sudden halt.

Her horse gave a *whinny* of protest and reared up, but Syre clung on, then brought the horse back under control.

After she'd led the horse in several ever-tightening circles to calm it down, she felt the horse's mood cool, and she turned her attention onto Lou.

In her surprise at seeing Lou out and about—*not* locked away in his stuffy Throne Room—she almost missed the fact that Lou's companion *wasn't* Flucknor at all.

It was Guilknot.

Lou's personal errand boy . . . though, to call him a *boy* now when he was easily the same age as Syre seemed somewhat strange.

She took in Guilknot's bony appearance, his pale skin, and how, although there was no doubt that his body was twice the size of the waif he'd once been, he hadn't ever really ground into it fully.

His eyes and nose and mouth seemed several sizes too small for his *man's* face.

For a few seconds, Syre found herself thinking about Flucknor, and where *he* might be.

Syre remained seated on her horse while Lou approached her.

He wore a stern expression. His straw-coloured hair was thinning about the fringe, and at the centre of his scalp. And he had deep, dark bags tugging at the base of his eye sockets. He approached Syre warily. She knew that he used a horse out of necessity, and that he had *always* been secretly afraid of them.

Syre parted her lips to speak, but before she got a chance, Lou cut her off.

"Why're you following us?" Lou said.

"I . . ." Syre just about got out.

"Turn around," he said, and then, returning to his own horse, and to Guilknot, he added, "*Now!*"

Syre felt a weight form in the centre of her chest. She watched on as Lou and Guilknot mounted their horses once more. Although Lou surely believed that he hid his fear of horses well, that he showed no outward signs of terror, *she*—at least—could make out the slight twitch in his eye as he took up the reins.

As Lou turned to Guilknot, clearly to inform him that they were going to continue on their way, Syre knew that she wouldn't stay silent.

That she wouldn't *allow* Lou to force her into silence.

"What're you doing?" Syre said, her voice crisp and cool, devoid of the frustrated emotion that Lou had communicated to her with his order for her to leave.

Lou didn't look back at her. He kept his head turned to Guilknot, his voice remaining low, impossible for Syre to hear. When Lou had finished saying whatever it was that he had said, Guilknot seized hold of the reins of his horse, turned sharply, and headed off onward along the narrow passageway, leaving Lou and Syre alone.

Only now did Lou turn back to Syre. "It's none of your business," Lou replied.

Syre met Lou's eyes, stared hard back at them. Then she broke from her silence. "Why're you having Flucknor follow me?" she said. "Why're you keeping an *eye* on me?"

Lou gave Syre an equally cool stare in return. "Because it's for the security of the Kingdom," he replied.

Syre almost burst out in laughter at hearing that.

But she restrained herself.

"Please," she said, "it's because I'm your little sister, isn't it? You're afraid of me going wandering off, of me getting myself into trouble." She paused for a long moment and then added, "You're secretly afraid that I might—*one night*—slip out of the Palace and never return. That I'll run away."

Lou's silence spoke volumes.

He continued to stare at her sternly.

Syre noticed that she could no longer hear the hoofs of Guilknot's horse.

Wherever he and Lou were headed, they'd coordinated ahead of time.

With an exaggerated squeezing of his thighs on his horse's flanks, Lou brought his horse toward Syre's, walking along calmly. But Syre could see, in the horse's eyes, that Lou didn't retain total control. That the horse *knew* if it wanted—if it *really* wanted—it could break away from its rider; leave him on his backside in the middle of the cobblestones.

King or not.

When Lou was right beside her, their horses beside one another, so that he might've reached out and grabbed hold of her if he'd wished to, he lowered his voice to a husky whisper, and said, "Go back to the Palace—we'll speak about this later."

Without waiting for her reply, Lou gave his horse another tug of the reins and trotted off after Guilknot.

Syre watched on as he disappeared around the corner, and then listened to the hoofs of his horse as he put distance between the two of them.

She thought long and hard about returning to the Palace.

About doing what he said.

But she had done just what he said for so long.

And she was tired of it.

Decided, she brought the reins down on her horse's neck, gave it a squeeze with her thighs. And she knew that although she and her brother shared the same blood, they were nothing alike.

A BROTHEL AT NIGHT

Sheilds lay back in bed, his hands clasped on his stomach. His quarters were tight. No windows. Barely space for the straw mattress dropped, with haste, into the middle of the room. As he felt his thoughts stirring within his mind, he tried his best to relax, to allow his brain to take him away somewhere else.

But when he allowed that to happen, it only took him back to Onderswort.

To the prison colony where he had spent the best part of two decades.

He could still smell the excrement, and the stench of piss which clung to everything.

He recalled how, whenever he would draw a breath, he would taste that musky unpleasantness at the back of his throat. He never grew accustomed to it, and every time he experienced the sensation—even simply *thinking* about the sensation now—he felt as if he might turn over on his side and vomit his guts out.

Since Sheilds had nothing except for the crimson tunic and beige pair of trousers his brother Jhang had presented him with, that was all he wore now.

He could feel his heart throbbing away in his chest, constantly on the lookout for danger, expecting to cease its beating at any second—to have a merciful blade slipped through it, bringing it to a halt forever.

In the near distance, he heard the sound of moaning, the grunts and groans of the clientele, of those who frequented the brothel. And the fishy, sweet smell of *love* seemed to cling to everything; although an effort had obviously been made to cover it with some sort of fruity perfume.

Sheilds had never really seen the point of the physical act of love. He had never really been able to see humans as anything more than lumps of meat.

For him, in a way, he could imagine no other explanation for having survived Onderswort. For having managed to *escape* Onderswort.

When Sheilds had taken up his post tonight—his first night of work—the woman, who'd introduced herself, *coldly*, as Diagham, had told him that it wouldn't be necessary for him to stand on the door; and that she would call for help if she needed any.

Sheilds hadn't complained.

Following his brother Jhang's threats, Diagham had already paid Sheilds his first week of wages. He had made all the vital purchases: vegetables, fruits, hunks of meat to cook with; and then he had set his mind to the tools of his trade:

The knives.

It sent a quiver of excitement through Sheilds's gut just to think about them all now; spread out on the market stall, their blades glinting in the sunlight. Their edges sharpened for cutting through skin, maybe *bone too*, if Sheilds found himself getting carried away.

Already, he found himself thinking about it.

About *what* he did.

The cloth.

Skin.

Blood.

Then the *bone.*

Just allowing those thoughts to drift through his brain sent him almost wild. As he listened in to the groans of the clientele, the magnified *shrieks* of the prostitutes, he clamoured for someone to call for help. To call for him to do what he did best.

To call for him to *kill.*

It was as Sheilds was on the verge of sleep that he heard what he'd been waiting for.

The sound cut through the groans and moans of pleasure.

And then one authentic, shrill scream of humanity resounded throughout the dreary pit.

As Sheilds felt gentle, warm beads of sweat trickle down his forehead, he wished he might've had more of an opportunity to select his tool.

In the end, the call had come so suddenly, and Sheilds had acted so out of instinct, that he had snatched up the first knife he had laid hand on.

This particular knife was one of the larger ones and had a crooked blade, and gnarled teeth for *tearing.* Despite its serviceable blade, the reason why Sheilds had been most attracted to it had more to do with the handle.

It was made of some sort of bone; what bone it exactly might be, Sheilds wasn't entirely sure.

But it had drawn him in all the more.

He loved items which were crafted from the bare essentials of existence; the building blocks from which all of them were made of when it came down to it.

When the concepts of rank, place, *stature* were wiped clean, they would all be nothing more than browning, yellowing bones in the ground.

He couldn't care *less* what wise men and women said about an afterlife.

For Sheilds, humans were nothing more than animals.

And they would suffer the same fate.

Buried in the ground.

A feast for the worms.

Sheilds sprinted along the corridor, glad now to think that Onder-swort had kept his body thin and mean, while all those around him—those from his childhood; those he'd grown up with—had become doughy and contented in their middle age.

He held the knife down at his side and fancied that he already had the coppery scent of blood lingering in his nostrils. He would enjoy this. He would *really* enjoy this.

Sheilds stopped briefly, listened for the sound. Although there were no more cries for help, he could still sense the snatched breaths coming from nearby. He ducked into a small room off the corridor. It was covered, floor to ceiling, with plumped-up velvet cushions: all of them the same crimson shade as the tunic which Sheilds wore.

But the room itself was empty.

He shifted on quickly, feeling his pulse pound harder, the blood running hot and thick about his veins. It pressed him onward. To be faster. To make his feet lighter.

When he reached another room, he found that, too, was bare.

And the next.

But, when he finally came to the second-to-last doorway off the corridor, he realised he had found his place.

He peered in through the doorway, seeing a four-poster bed there; one which seemed as if it might've been more in place in Ilsnare Palace than in a common brothel.

It had pink-shaded netted curtains hanging down from the posters which left the figures on the bed in a silhouette. Unlike Sheilds's own room, there was a window here, but it had the shutters drawn.

Still hearing the stifled breathing, and the sounds of struggle, Sheilds moved quickly. He swept back the netted curtain of the four-poster bed to reveal the pair of naked figures within.

When the netted curtain swept back into his vision, he tore it down off its rail, allowed it to tumble into a heap at his feet.

Instinctively, his eyes moved over the bare breasts of the prostitute. She had long blond hair and gaping, blue eyes which glared back at him.

Sheilds saw that the client had his hands about her throat.

Acting faster than he could think, Sheilds leaped at the client, knocked him flat on his back, on the bed, then pressed the blade of the knife to his throat. Through gritted teeth, Sheilds said what he had so many times before. "You move—even and *inch*—and I'll cut you open."

It felt as if Sheilds lay on the client for hours, the blade touching his throat, ready to press down hard at any moment; to snuff the life out of him.

But Sheilds held back.

Something held him back.

The client stared out at him with bulging eyes.

There was something . . . something about . . .

Sheilds felt somebody tugging on the sleeve of his tunic.

His first reaction was to shuttle his elbow back, to knock them away.

But the person was insistent.

So insistent that Sheilds was forced to shift his attention away from the client, and onto the person who was pulling him away. He saw that it was the blond prostitute. And that her mouth was jabbering away, telling him off about something. Soon enough, he realised what she said, he managed to penetrate the thick Ilsnare dialect which'd become almost alien since his time away.

"Stop! Stop! Let. Him. *GO!*"

Sheilds held onto the client for another few seconds and then, after jabbing the blade of his knife in just enough to give the man the sliver of a cut, he backed off.

And the blond prostitute released him.

Sheilds pushed himself up off the bed, and got back onto his feet. He glanced to the prostitute, naked, on all fours, her bare bottom facing him as she cooed over the client, lying back on the pillows, a bloody trickle running down his throat.

The blond prostitute turned back to Sheilds, her mouth twisted and lines engrained in her forehead. "You *idiot!*" she said. "You've *hurt* him. Just what in hell's name do you think you were doing?!"

Sheilds couldn't find the words.

He had only been doing his job.

He had heard what he'd interpreted to be a cry for help and he had come running.

He had played the *hero.*

And yet, he had done wrong.

Messed up.

As always seemed to happen when he went by the rules.

"You!"

Sheilds turned around, looked to the doorway.

He saw that Diagham stood there, the woman with the prematurely grey hair. The one who had accepted him here . . . albeit under some strenuous threats.

She nodded to the scene on the bed behind Sheilds. "What's going on here?" she said. "Why're you in here?"

Finally having caught his breath, Sheilds replied, "I thought I heard sounds of trouble—so I came running . . . I thought she was in distress."

"Does she *look* in distress to you?"

Sheilds followed the accusatory finger which Diagham stretched out. He looked back to the bed, and to the blond prostitute crouching over the naked client.

Something about the scene tickled Sheilds in an odd way.

He decided that it was some sort of déjà vu.

He seemed to have a memory of having killed a naked couple while they lay in one another's arms—believing themselves safe . . .

Sheilds shook his head at Diagham's question. "No," he said, his voice sombre, low.

"Well, then," Diagham said, "what're you doing here?"

Sheilds had no reply to this.

It was almost like being back in court, facing up to the Galleries of Justice, and how he hadn't been allowed to give a satisfying answer. No matter how truthful it was.

That was how he'd got sent to Onderswort.

That was what had made him what he was today:

A monster.

The blond prostitute glanced back at Sheilds, then looked to Diagham. "He made him *bleed*, Diage."

Diagham stared at Sheilds long and hard, and then she gave a shake of her head. "I want you out of here," she said, "and I want you out tonight. I couldn't care less about those threats. In my opinion it's more of a danger to have you here than to possibly face the consequences of some *retaliation*."

And with that, an apologetic look to the client—whose cut, Sheilds was a touch disappointed to note, had stopped bleeding—Diagham slipped from the room and away. Back to whichever bedroom served as her office.

Sheilds made to leave the room behind; he had made a disgrace of himself. His brother had done his best for him, under the circumstances, and Sheilds had ruined it all after a matter of only hours.

"Wait."

Sheilds lingered in the doorway, wondering what fresh misery he might find himself in for. This time it was the client who spoke. He—*apparently*—wasn't so taken aback by a little rough treatment. Sheilds turned back, looked to the client for the first time properly:

He looked to the jowls; the small-lipped mouth.

Those vaguely *mean* eyes.

He had tufts of curly white hair sticking out from his crown in a semi-circle.

And then, because Sheilds felt as if he should avert his gaze, he turned his attention downward, to the man's hands. Saw that he had perfectly manicured fingernails.

Surely this was some sort of government official.

That would be *just* Sheilds's luck.

"Don't I know you?" the client said.

Sheilds gave a doleful shake of his head and was about to add that he'd been out of town for a long while, before catching himself—telling himself that that *certainly wouldn't* be anything like a good idea. It wouldn't take a giant leap of logic to realise that Sheilds could well be some sort of a criminal on the run . . . let alone an escapee from Onderswort.

The client narrowed his eyes. He propped himself up in bed, apparently not too bothered about being stark naked now. Perhaps he was thinking through some sort of punishment for Sheilds:

Hanging?

Flogging?

Stoning?

. . . It would be a mercy in a way.

Death.

"No," the client said, eyes still narrowed, lips pursed, "I *do* know you."

Sheilds felt his chest tighten. He gripped his knife all the tighter. He stared back into the eyes of the client. He had nothing to lose now. If he had to kill the man then so be it. Sheilds wasn't prepared to give up his well-won liberty so easily.

In fact, they would have to pry it out from between his cold, dead fingers.

"You're Sheilds Guider, aren't you?"

Sheilds flinched to hear his family name tagged onto his given name. Since his father had never been present, and their mother refused to use his name once he had *gone*, she'd decided to use the street where their home was situated as the family surname.

It made Sheilds feel a little like a bumpkin.

As if he was nothing more than a cockroach.

Because, with no name, there was no history.

It was almost a second reaction which told him that he needed to run; that this man had rumbled him. And that he was going to get himself sent back to Onderswort if he didn't leave *right now* . . . if he didn't *kill* the man and his lover *right now.*

And yet Sheilds was unsure what'd come over him.

He remained stock still.

"Don't you recognise me?" the man said. "It's Tineoots Pottler."

All of a sudden, the sinister thoughts which'd ploughed through Sheilds's mind gave way. He felt something like *tenderness* make itself felt in his chest. "Tineoots?" he said, hardly able to believe it.

Sheilds was dimly aware of the blond prostitute giving a sigh, apparently bored with this conversation she had no stock in, and carting herself up off the bed, trudging her way out of the bedroom with a sheet wrapped about her body.

Sheilds's mind switched back, to his childhood, to the children who he'd known growing up.

They'd been a gang—*of sorts*—and Tineoots, well, he had been a member.

After that they'd all gone their own way.

Sheilds had gone his; and Tineoots—*apparently*—had gone his.

Tineoots was smiling widely now, his lips glistening. The narrow cut at his throat continued to ooze with blood but it no longer spilled drops. "I suppose you're in search of a job," he said.

Sheilds felt his chest tighten slightly.

All those bloody-minded thoughts which'd risen up in him seemed to dissipate now; to crumble away. "Yes," Sheilds said, his throat impossibly dry.

Tineoots continued to smile back at him, and then gave him a sturdy nod. "I might be able to help with that, if you like."

NIGHT AT ILSNARE PALACE

S yre sat up on the brick wall which surrounded the paddock area of the stables in Ilsnare Palace. Her eyes didn't leave the gates for one second. She couldn't even *imagine* what Tineoots might say if he saw her here—*at this hour*—out in the dark, lurking about the back end of the Palace.

The cold night air would be enough of a reason for Tineoots to *demand* that she return indoors.

But Syre enjoyed the gentle bite of the winter air, the way that her breath formed clouds before her face. How it tended to heighten her sense of smell and taste; as if she was living on some higher plane.

As if she could constantly use her magic without wearing herself out.

Sometimes she wondered how it might feel to give herself up totally to her magic—to *lose* the control which Lou was constantly going on about her *keeping*.

The thought sent a tingle down her spine.

She had no idea how Lou had managed it.

She had taken off after him, galloped her horse along in the direction she was *certain* he'd been headed. But she hadn't been able to locate him. She'd lost him among the labyrinth of streets and been forced to return to the Palace.

Once she'd got down one back alley, she'd even transformed herself into a crow to see if she might be able to track him that way. But she hadn't seen anything in the surrounding area.

It was as if Lou had up and disappeared into thin air.

"Evening."

Syre glanced to her side and saw that Flucknor was there.

He was wearing a light-blue tunic over the top of some riding trousers. His tunic matched the colour of his eyes. He had on a pair of leather boots tugged all the way up the backs of his calves.

"I can see you've been out on the town," Syre replied, turning her attention back to the gates, expecting them to fly open at any second.

Flucknor hauled himself up the brick wall and took his seat beside her. He met her gaze and looked off to the gates. "Who're you waiting for?" he said.

"You know," Syre replied.

Flucknor said nothing else.

Despite feeling a strong urge to press her lips up against his—to kiss him *hard*—Syre held herself back. She hated being left out of whatever *important* things were going on . . . almost as much as she hated being tied down to Ilsnare Palace; having to play the Good Little Princess.

Although she was young, she'd learned that one of the most effective ways to assert power over Flucknor was to deny him her affections. Doing that made him *anxious* and she could make him do almost anything she could imagine.

Could make him *say* almost anything she could imagine.

"Where'd Lou go?" Syre said, feeling Flucknor inching himself closer to her, and pulling away from him.

Flucknor pressed his lips together then shook his head. "No idea," he said, "he tends to tell me about as much as he tells you."

"Except for the Webbing Armoury," Syre shot back. "You know where it is—*don't you?*"

Flucknor gave up his advances.

He retreated back, noticing that Syre wasn't going to give him what he wanted until she had something of her own. "Listen," he said, "I *really* don't . . . Lou, sometimes he asks me to do things for him, but they have nothing to do with the Webbing Armoury." He shrugged, then looked off to the gates. "You know how it is, he doesn't believe in sharing the location with any other mage—let alone a pair of ice mages like the two of us."

"He doesn't trust us," Syre replied.

Flucknor remained silent for a long few moments. "No, he doesn't. But, if it makes you feel any better, I don't think that he trusts *any- one*—not anymore." He shook his head to himself. "When you've experienced the type of power that Lou has, when you've become the Spider Warrior, I don't suppose you want anybody else to ex- perience it."

Syre scoffed. "And why'd you think that is? Is he worried that, somehow, we're going to seize it, use it against him? Use it to cause chaos?"

"I think it's simpler than that," Flucknor replied, "I think it's just that he doesn't want to see any more suffering—any more *pain* .. . he wants to keep peace in Shellacnass for as long as he can pos- sibly manage."

Syre felt a touch of petulance rise in her; a sort of bitterness catching at the back of her throat. "What's so great about peace, anyway?" she said. "Where's the adventure—where's the *ambi- tion* to better ourselves; to better our position?"

Even as Syre muttered the words, she felt as if she'd said too much; even to someone who she held as much confidence in as Flucknor.

These were the sorts of thoughts which would come to her late at night, as she lay in bed—*alone*—wondering at her position in the world.

"And what would 'ambition' achieve," Flucknor replied. "What would *war* achieve?"

Syre thought about how Flucknor had witnessed the monastery of Ravensbark, where he'd previously lived as a monk, crumble down—become a casualty in a magical war.

He, more than anybody else, knew adventure. And he had witnessed ambition first hand.

The ambition of Ma'reygar.

Sometimes, when she thought about it, she wondered just how bad Ma'reygar's world really would've been. His will had been for magic to rule Shellacnass.

Sure, the Mortals might've had reason to fear, but things would've been immeasurably better for those who had magic running through their blood. No longer would they have to hide out in the shadowy corners of the night to practise—as Syre frequently did.

They wouldn't need to live like second-class citizens, unable to use what was their very strongest of powers.

If a Mortal—one such as Tineoots—decided to cause some sort of conflict with Syre then she could use whatever she saw fit to fight back.

Rather than reserve it as some sort of a last resort.

She felt that—if only she might be allowed—she could be *so much* stronger than what she was right now.

And getting her hands on the Webbing Armoury might well be the first step.

She was nothing like her brother.

She knew that, after all these years.

Whereas he had a Human's mind, she had a *crow's* mind.

Syre turned her attention back onto the gates of the stables.

Could she hear the *clop* of horse hoofs approaching?

The snorting exhales?

Flucknor reached out and took hold of her hand before she had a chance to resist him—to keep up this game she was playing. She turned to look at him, to meet his sweet, soft blue eyes. "Come on," he said, "let's go inside—we'll catch a cold out here."

Syre turned her attention back to the gates of the stables, as if Lou might romp right into the Palace right here and now.

But they didn't stir.

And, feeling an especially fierce, whipping, chilling wind, she acquiesced.

THE VIRTUE OF PATIENCE

Syre sat slumped on the Throne of Shellacnass waiting for her brother to return.

When a member of the House Staff entered the Throne Room and attempted to light up one of the torches, Syre chased him away, telling him that she preferred to remain in darkness.

Flucknor had long ago gone off to bed—become bored of the waiting game.

But Syre was more resilient.

She had things to talk to Lou about, and she was determined to be heard.

She rested her elbow on the arm of the throne, with her chin propped up on her fist.

When she finally heard the *patter* of footsteps coming closer, along the corridor, she suddenly caught a second wind, felt wide awake. She straightened up on the throne and thought through what she was going to say to her brother.

She would say what was on her mind.

Nothing more, nothing less.

There were things that he needed to hear.

She breathed in deeply, feeling the prickle of ice in her veins; her magic warning her that another like herself was approaching. She focussed her attention on the doorway to the Throne Room, silently urging her brother to come on in.

To confront her.

To have to answer her questions.

When Lou did appear in the doorway, his posture was ragged, and his complexion she could see, even in the darkness, was pallid—*beaten up.*

All at once, Syre felt the anger which'd been brewing in her fade. She thought about all he had done. All that he had *achieved* in his life. And the mighty warrior mage he had become . . . if only for a short while.

Apparently expecting confrontation himself, Lou gave her a hardy expression, and he pitched his voice at a growl when he spoke to her. "What'd you want?" he said.

Despite his anger-spiked words, Syre felt tenderness overwhelming her. She got up off the throne and trod toward Lou. Her heart dipped down into her stomach to see him like this; so clearly exhausted by his day's travails.

"Come on," she said, "I'll have the House Staff run you a warm bath."

At first she thought that Lou would bat away this offer, that he would act all *resilient* and storm off to his bedroom. But he said nothing, clearly too tired to so much as speak.

He simply gave a vague nod of acceptance.

Once the bath had been poured, and two female members of the House Staff had retreated to their quarters for the night, Syre knelt down at the side of the stone bath, watching Lou in profile.

She felt the hard press of the tiles at her kneecaps, the cramp working its way up her thighs.

But she tried not to think about it.

She felt sore, too, from the horse riding earlier in the day; though she was certain, however sore she felt herself, that Lou would feel equally so . . . having spent the entirety of his time riding with Guilknot.

Steam rose up into the air, meeting with the cool draught which blew in through the open door of the bathroom. As the steam rose, it curled in on itself, almost like a wave retreating back into the ocean.

Syre thought about her and Lou's journey out to Irmlesbrook, and how Lou had been terribly seasick throughout the entire trip.

That seemed like such a long time in the past now.

An adventure in another life.

Looking at her brother's face in profile, seeing the mucky water roll down his face and land in the bath, she couldn't help but think that he had peaked. That his youth had been stolen from him by forces much greater than himself.

By *war*.

And by *ambition*.

All those stupid things which Syre had said out loud.

She vaguely hoped that Flucknor wouldn't mention them to Lou, because, although Flucknor often tried to play down his relationship with Lou, Syre well knew that Flucknor was one of his most trusted allies.

And that they spoke freely; one with the other.

Syre was unsure whether or not Flucknor had told Lou about her and Flucknor's relationship. But surely Lou had heard the whispered rumours about the Palace. With a House Staff the size it was in Ilsnare Palace, the truth of the matter was that nothing remained a secret for very long.

Especially a concealed romance.

But Lou himself had never said anything about it to *her* . . . although, admittedly, these days, they hardly saw one another—let alone *spoke.*

As Lou reclined in the bath, Syre studied the prominent creases ingrained about his eyes.

Rooted deeply in his skin.

She could tell that there was worry there—*anxiety*—and she would've liked nothing more than to know what it was. To help unburden him.

But she knew, even now, that he saw her as little more than his baby sister. To be protected. To be *shielded* from all of the exterior horrors.

She certainly wasn't a *confidante.*

But, at the very least, she could *comfort* him.

He allowed her that.

Perhaps women *did* have some use for Lou after all.

About half an hour must've passed before Lou said anything. And it took Syre aback so much that she felt herself flinch slightly at the silence being broken so suddenly.

"Do you remember," Lou said, his voice stretched—*weak*, "when I returned home from the fields without my winter's supplement?"

Syre sketched her mind back.

If the encampments had seemed another life—if when Sully and Rut had been with them seemed like another life—then this was *yet another* altogether.

Almost as if it was a time before Syre had really come into being.

She nodded in reply.

Lou's face remained neutral, his weathered—*emaciated*—perspiring skin not giving off signals of any kind. Not betraying any sort of emotion. "I was so afraid," he said. "I was *paralysed* with fear—about what might happen to us; about what might happen to the family."

Syre thought back to her family, when they had lived in Endmere. She had heard that the whole village—along with others: Quagsmile, Gwindermere—had been rebuilt out of the ashes. When she had been given the offer of going on a Royal Visit; to be escorted by members of the Royal Guards out to the north of Ilsnare, she had refused.

She had told herself, at first, that it had been in keeping with her wish *not* to fulfil 'royal' obligations . . . but she later realised—when she caught herself shaking for apparently no reason in her bathroom later that day—the reason she didn't go was because she was *afraid* of returning.

Of going back to see the damage.

She could still recall how Lou had saved her. How the two of them had managed to escape the village by going out through the supply tunnel to *The Mocker's Pit*: the town's public house. Even back then, Syre could remember thinking that at least *some* use had been given to *The Mocker's Pit* beyond her and Lou's father getting himself sodden drunk every other night.

Lou's lips moved silently now, and his eyes fluttered to a close. She could just about make out the words he said. "I was . . . I was . . . so . . . so *afraid* . . ."

Syre reached out and caught Lou as he slid down, into the murky water of the stone bathtub.

Sometimes her own strength surprised her, how she was able to put her mind to the task of lugging this or that . . . but, then again, she supposed that throughout the decade they had spent at Ilsnare Palace her brother's muscles had only atrophied, and he had lost all traces of fat about his body. He was nothing but skin and bone now.

"Let's get you to bed," Syre said, with a slight smile; helping the dozing Lou back up from the surface of the bath water.

Even as she did help Lou up and out of the bath, Syre couldn't help wondering to herself what might've happened if she'd stood by, watched her brother sink below the surface of the water.

If she'd just slipped out of the bathroom.

Gone to bed.

Nobody would've been any the wiser.

Her brother might've drowned.

And she would've become *Queen.*

PURSUIT

As **Sheilds felt** the morning rays of the sun against his face, warming his body from the outside-in, he gazed along the backstreets of Ilsnare.

He was currently located in a side alley off the Crystal Causeway, among the mazy streets which surrounded Ilsnare Palace; the much-celebrated strategic feat which made a grand assault on the Palace all but impossible . . . if the attacking forces even managed to get past the City Walls.

He glanced up the stone walls of the houses, to the slits in the stonework, where citizens could stick out their bows, or their crossbows, and rain all manner of hell down on those who sieged the city.

To think that, if he had been a soldier in one of those attacking forces, he would be *easily* shot dead right where he stood.

Thankfully, though, he hadn't become a soldier.

He had come into Ilsnare as an individual, and he was determined that this was the condition by which he would live his life forever more.

Nothing about slaving away in an army appealed to him; even now looking back on the option the judge had given him: to join the Army of Shellacnass, or to be sent to Onderswort.

He would've chosen Onderswort each and every time.

After all, Onderswort had brought him back here, hadn't it?

And better that, better to cling to whatever semblance of *life* remained within him, than to be lying dead on some faraway battlefield; the long grasses growing up over him, the rats scavenging his armour, picking at what little flesh continued to cling to his bones.

Sheilds glanced up along the street, then swore to himself.

There was no sign of the man he was supposed to be surveying.

Sheilds backed away from the street stall he had been feigning interest in, and tossed the half-eaten apple he'd been chomping on away across the cobblestones. As he chewed on the sweet apple flesh in his mouth, he quickened his pace, swept his dark-brown cloak out of the way of his feet, so that he could walk freely.

Hearing the owner of the stall jabbering on in his ear, imploring him to pay the going rate for the apple he'd just consumed, Sheilds dipped his fingers into the inside pocket of his cloak and, from the drawstring purse he kept concealed within—well out of reach of the Crystal City's famed pickpockets—he tossed several grung back over his shoulder.

He listened to the coins clink as they landed on the cobblestones behind him, and told himself that he would be far away before the owner of the stall realised that they were forgeries.

When Tineoots had given him this job—when Tineoots had offered him this position within the Crystal City spy network known as the Eye—he had also given him a good supply of fake coins.

Tineoots had informed Sheilds that this was a good measure to keep the citizens of the Crystal City's suspicions raised against the outside; against the foreign world beyond the walls of Ilsnare.

It was some tangible means for them to see the threat against them; the ill will coming to bear on their everyday lives.

A way in which the Eye could aid the continuation of the status quo all throughout the Crystal City.

Because who else would falsify monies but a foreigner?

Sheilds had little-to-no interest in politics; he was a man very much invested in self-interest, but even he admired the grand scale of this conceit.

And, he had to admit, his respect for his old childhood friend—Tineoots—had only grown; and to think that he was a trusted member of the Royal Court itself. That he stood on ceremony within the walls of Ilsnare Palace with nobody the wiser. An agent for the Council of Wisemen; someone to keep tabs on the King of Shellacnass twenty-four hours a day.

Sheilds paced on more quickly. He turned the corner.

Still no sign of the man he was supposed to pursue.

He had to admit that, when Tineoots had first offered him this job—weeks ago now—when Tineoots had asked him to be a Watcher, Sheilds had believed it would be mundane work; that he would soon tire of trailing people's heels; of clinging to the night-time shadows without the climax of a murder to follow.

Strangely, though, he had found it *compelling.*

To skirt the periphery of somebody's vision, to remain concealed, and then to file a cryptic report—to scribble down his observations on a piece of parchment which he handed over, folded in two, to a wise woman who ran a stall of curiosities on the Crystal Causeway.

Perhaps this had been Sheilds's calling all along.

And it had taken him this much time in his life to realise it.

Finally, having arrived in a deserted lane, Sheilds caught sight of the man he was pursuing. He eyed the light-blue tunic.

Took in the shoulder-length, silver-blond hair hoiked into a ponytail which bobbed as he strolled along.

As always with his assignments for the Eye, Sheilds was only ever given the information he *needed* to know; often only a description of the subject to be surveyed, and what exactly he was supposed to be making note of:

Locations travelled to.

Types of people spoken with.

Objects purchased . . . even, on occasion, he was given the freedom to speculate as to the mental state of the subject. Were they angered, frustrated, *anxious?*

Sheilds reported it all.

He closed on the target, only twenty paces away now.

And that was when the target glanced back, over his shoulder.

Caught sight of him.

And broke into a run.

Sheilds stood stock still.

He was under very specific orders when it came to having his cover blown. He was to simply slip away—into a crowd, if at all possible—and to regroup.

To abandon surveillance for the day.

He knew, from experience, the couple of times that he *thought* he'd been spotted by the subject, that he wouldn't be given the same assignment again.

He understood it from the Eye's point of view, that they didn't want to arouse unnecessary suspicion in the subject; and that they, most likely, would select a Watcher of an entirely different physical profile the next time.

Sheilds had to admit that he found this aspect of the job immensely frustrating.

Since dawn, Sheilds had been camped out on the Crystal Causeway, breathing in the stale, fishy stench of the River Ils, waiting for the subject to show himself. And when he had, Sheilds had felt something approaching the excitement—the *adrenaline*—which entered his bloodstream when anticipating the nearing of a murder.

And now, after a solid few hours of pursuing the subject, of making mental notes on his movements, his state of mind, he would have to give it all up . . . but, what if . . . what if he *kept* on pursuing him . . . what if he cornered him . . . *really* got some answers . . .

Before Sheilds could stop himself—as so often happened when he smelled blood coiling up his nostrils—he acted. He broke into a run.

Set his mind to pursuing the subject.

Sheilds's feet remained light after the years and years he'd spent in Onderswort; and he could easily outrun men half his age. A good thing too, given that he'd had the need for such an ability on more than one occasion.

He pursued the subject down another series of narrow lanes, skirting the cobblestones with the soles of the rugged leather boots which Tineoots had presented him as a sort of welcome gift to his service to the Eye.

Finally, he cornered the subject, got him stuck down a dead end street.

Wooden boxes of flowers hung down from the stonework; and Sheilds breathed in the heady, sweet scents. He could taste his own sweat in his mouth, and could feel a couple of beads of sweat rolling their way down his brow.

The sun beamed down into this tiny lane, off the Crystal Causeway.

The subject stood still glaring back at him, his shoulders rising and falling with his brisk breathing.

Without any conscious thought, Sheilds reached into his cloak and felt for the knife which he kept there. Knowing better than to draw it in searing daylight, he only hovered his fingers over it, ready to draw it out at a moment's notice.

But the subject didn't seem keen to put up any sort of a fight.

Sheilds approached the subject, feeling his heart beat steadily. His thoughts came to him calmly—*easily* understood. When he was no more than ten or fifteen paces away from the subject he stood still and stared.

Finally, the subject spoke to him, eyes wide, arms prone at about chest height, as if he might need to fight Sheilds off. "What'd you *want?*" the subject said.

Sheilds raised a smirk and then withdrew the knife from within his cloak.

This particular knife was one he had acquired only last week.

More of a needle than a blade, really.

If he'd been asked to guess after its origin then he might've placed it as coming from one of those settlements in the foot-hills of the Sable Mountains—some out-of-the-way village where they specialised in elaborate designs. And yet this, the needle-like point at the end of the leather grip, was certainly the sort of weapon more at home in a large settlement than a small, backwater village.

The perfect tool for handling in a crowd—for sticking someone with and then simply walking away.

But it was important that the subject *see* the weapon.

That he *fear* Sheilds.

Sheilds observed the subject's attention drift away from his face and down to the weapon which Sheilds held at his side.

That was good.

Right where he *wanted* the subject to look.

Without Sheilds saying anything more, the subject dug about within his light-blue tunic, and he produced a pouch of coins. He held it out to Sheilds, offering it to him. "Here," he said, "this is all I've got on me—if you need more then let me know . . . I can *get* you more, but I don't have it on me now."

Sheilds eyed the pouch for the couple of moments it took to decide that—*really*—he wasn't interested in petty cash. He got all the petty cash he needed from his connections with the Eye . . . and, forged, or not, it was more than enough to meet his needs.

What use did Sheilds have for money?

Sheilds took a couple of steps forward, approaching the pouch of coins. He reached out for it, and then, with a swift motion, knocked the pouch clean out of the subject's fist.

It landed at Sheilds's feet with a satisfying *clink.*

Sheilds didn't so much as look down at the coins. Instead, he reached out his needle and held it to the fleshy part of the subject's throat.

The subject recoiled but did not take a step backward.

That was good for the subject.

Sometimes Sheilds couldn't control himself when they *resisted.*

"Who are you?" Sheilds said, his voice gruff, to the point.

The subject glared back at him over the top of the needle Sheilds held to his throat. His eyes squirmed about in their sockets, clearly searching for a means of escape.

But he wouldn't escape.

Not yet.

Not until Sheilds had got the answers he required for his report.

"Fluck . . . Fluck*nor* . . ." the subject finally got out.

Sheilds thought about prompting him for his surname, but decided that the subject might well be like himself. That he had *never had* a surname . . . not his father's name, in any case.

"What're you doing?" Sheilds said, and then, thinking again, he rephrased the question, "Where're you *going?*"

The subject—*Flucknor*—remained still, the nib of the needle drawing a rivulet of blood which trickled down his neck.

Flucknor shook his head.

His eyes became watery

No—*please*—he wasn't going to cry, was he?

Sheilds could hardly handle it when they *cried* . . . and much less when they got down on their knees in that pathetic way they did.

Begging for their lives.

As if their life was Sheilds's to give them.

From that second on, everything moved quickly, too quickly for Sheilds to fathom.

Sheilds was aware of a burning—*cold*—sensation.

Right in the centre of his forehead.

At first, he attempted to ignore it, to keep the nib of the needle pointed at Flucknor's throat. But, soon enough, the sensation wracked the whole of Flucknor's body.

An uncontrollable shaking seized hold of him.

It tightened his muscles and fired his nerves.

He felt the fiery cold feeling enter his bloodstream, and rattle about his veins, causing him to shake and then, in the distance, he was aware of the needle slipping out from between his fingers; of it clattering to the cobblestones, at his feet.

And then he felt himself tumble down, his bones no longer sufficient to keep the rest of his body upright.

He landed on the cobblestones with a damp *thud.*

The side of his head struck stone.

Stars spotted his vision.

And then his eyelids, apparently of their own volition, closed off the world to him.

When Sheilds came to once more, there was a group of children standing about him.

They wore rags, and were bare-footed.

Seeing his eye open, they backed up a couple of steps.

Sheilds's whole body felt stiff, unmoving.

Up above his head, he could see that the sky had turned the colour of flame, that the sun was retreating; that it was setting alight to the glass rooftops of Ilsnare.

He had been lying here all day . . . *stunned.*

With the boys staring on at him, Sheilds gradually eased himself back up to his feet.

He almost toppled right back over—but managed to keep his footing.

He trod away from the group of boys, from the street urchins, and he might've continued on his way, all the way back to the lodgings which Tineoots had arranged for him if it hadn't been for one of the boys calling him back.

"Mister? Mister?"

Sheilds glanced back over his shoulder to the boy who'd called out to him, and he saw, clutched there in his fist, was the needle which he'd held to the subject . . . *Flucknor's* . . . throat.

Still feeling uneasy on his feet, Sheilds approached the boy who held the needle out to him.

Sheilds took it off him, and replaced it in its sheath, concealed within his cloak. He even managed to give the boy a gentle smile. "Thank you," he said. "Very kind."

As he turned away from the stunned boys, from their stunned gazes, he paced out along the lane and thought about what had befallen him.

Why, there was no question about it.

He'd had a run-in with a mage.

A SECRET KEPT
IS A BURDEN TAKEN

S yre could feel the whole of her body trembling.

There had been an illness going around the Palace.

Like always, it had begun with the House Staff—with those who worked in the kitchen.

She recalled how she had heard the flat *cough-cough* of one of the servants there; and when Syre, chomping away at the beef which'd been served her, had told the young lady to take the rest of the day off, she had given Syre a delirious smile.

The young lady had had a sort of purple-blue complexion.

And dark bags beneath her eyes.

Sometimes, Syre had the urge to speak with Tineoots, to have him ease off on his staff; so that they didn't believe that they were compelled to work if they were feeling ill.

More than anything else, it was dangerous.

Illness, as Syre well knew from her time out in the wilderness, among a large travelling community, could soon spread. First it would take the young and the old; then move on, as if strengthening, to take the middle-aged; and the previously healthy.

Syre had no appetite for illness, but she was certain that was what befell her now.

With a couple of coughs, and still tasting the well-salted chicken broth she'd had brought to her chambers, she pulled on Lou's sheepskin cloak.

Since the night she'd snuck out to peek in on that meeting of the Outcast at *The Soore Whip*, that night when she'd discovered that there were *Creatures* living among the citizens of Ilsnare, she hadn't thought to return the cloak.

And, since Lou hadn't asked for it back, she'd decided that it was now her own.

As she slipped it over her shoulders, she already felt the warmth of its thick, almost mother-like layers. All she wanted to do now was lie in bed and doze . . . she knew that whenever she eventually found sleep, her dreams would be giddy and strange.

Feverish.

She trod over to the glass balcony doors of her quarters, and peered out over the moonstruck cityscape.

She spied the playful, orange glows of the streetlights scattered about the streets of Ilsnare. And she saw the blurred, shadowy figures moving about the streets.

It still blew her mind to think about all the people who resided within Ilsnare; about how she was nothing more than a simple girl from one of the Northern Villages.

She found it difficult to comprehend the many lives—the daily routines—which must play out within the City Walls.

Here she was, only aware of a tiny pocket of activity; some corner of the city:

Ilsnare Palace.

Syre turned her attention to the courtyard below, and then to the figure who wandered in through the gates of the Palace. She watched on as the Royal Guards on duty down in the courtyard shifted a quick glance over the shadowy figure before nodding them through. As the figure came closer still, Syre recognised, from the slightly lagging gait, that it was Flucknor.

That Flucknor had been out and about in the city.

If Syre hadn't been feeling so under the weather she might've had the strength to feel something approaching anger—*anger* at his hypocrisy; that although Syre was well and truly banned from taking to the streets of Ilsnare after dark, it was perfectly acceptable for him to do the same.

Perhaps it was the knowledge that, in her current state, Syre would find it somewhat difficult to raise her magic against some unseemly foe . . . if the worst came to the worst and she was forced to fight off a mugger, or some other kind of assailant.

She needed bedrest.

To recuperate her strength.

Then she could handle such arguments.

But not wishing to go to bed *quite yet*—at least not before she had received a goodnight kiss from her 'beloved'—she slunk out of her chambers, and off into the Entrance Hall of the Palace.

She waited patiently, standing at the top of the stone staircase, waiting for the Interior Guards to open the doors to Flucknor.

When they did, and Syre felt the bitterly cold draught wafting about the Entrance Hall, she found herself struck down with a fresh series of shudders. Her throat felt tight and dry—and *swollen.*

But she was determined to have her goodnight kiss.

Flucknor rounded the door, dressed in his familiar light-blue tunic. His blue eyes sparkled with the torchlight of the hall, and, after a quick sweep of his surroundings, they came to rest on Syre's. He hinted a slight smile in her direction, and then made to slink away into the shadows of the Palace; apparently headed to his quarters.

Syre called out to him, as if he might've missed seeing her standing up on the staircase.

Flucknor curtailed his escape. He glanced back at her.

Met her eye for a moment.

Syre's gaze slipped downward, to his neck, and to the dark patch there. She furrowed her brow then approached Flucknor.

To begin with, Flucknor seemed so skittish—he seemed so *on edge*—that Syre believed he might attempt to slip out the Entrance Hall before she had a chance to get her long-promised goodnight kiss.

As she drew up to him, she got a proper look at the mark on his neck, at the blotch of dried blood.

She reached for the spot, ran her fingertips across the surface.

When she examined her hand, she saw that her skin was coated in blood.

"What is it?" she said. "What happened?"

Flucknor averted her gaze, looked back to the doors of the Entrance Hall, as if he was suddenly interested in the Royal Guards stationed there. He looked back to Syre with a slight grimace on his lips. "When I was out in the city today, a man, he tried to *mug* me."

"To 'mug' you?" Syre replied, feeling a touch of disbelief.

Flucknor nodded. "He cornered me down this deserted little lane. I offered him my purse, but . . ."

"What?"

Flucknor shrugged his shoulders then shook his head. He attempted a smile but it didn't linger too long on his lips. "Don't worry about it," he said. "I'm sure that it was my fault. For not being aware enough of my surroundings."

He turned away from her, apparently intending to head for his quarters.

But Syre was too fast for him.

She reached out and grabbed hold of the sleeve of his light-blue tunic.

Her strength surprised even her.

"I can heal that," Syre said.

Flucknor gazed back into her eyes—no trace of the forced smile any longer. "No," he said, "really, it's okay. I can hear from your voice that you're not feeling well. You should save your strength—plough all the energy you have into getting better."

Syre defied this claim without words, as she continued to clamp the sleeve of Flucknor's tunic with her fingers, keeping him from going. "Let me *heal* it," she said, more insistent this time, but keeping her voice low.

Just as Lou had been a few weeks back, when he'd returned from his day out—doing who knew *what*—Flucknor seemed too tired to protest.

Aware that the Royal Guards might be observing them, Syre tugged at the sleeve of Flucknor's tunic, moving him toward the stone staircase. At first he resisted, but he soon gave in, no longer having the strength to fight back.

She led him up the staircase, and was surprised to note that he was trembling.

Whatever had happened in the city, it had shaken him up something terrible.

HIDDEN DANGER

A few days later, when Syre arrived to the Throne Room, she was dismayed to see that Tineoots was there. She had hoped to find her brother Lou alone, but now she realised that he wasn't here at all.

Before she had a chance to duck back out of the Throne Room, Tineoots called out to her. "Princess Syre," he said, in that sing-song voice of his.

The one which Syre sometimes woke from nightmares hearing resounding within her skull.

Annoyed at having her quick escape thwarted, she turned back to Tineoots.

She put on her very best *Good Girl* smile.

Now she was glad that she had thought to put on a yellow-green dress; something which Tineoots would certainly have remarked on as being 'appropriate' for a princess. And she'd had the good sense to dab a little of the scented hazelnut oil about her ears and neck so that Tineoots wouldn't make some remark about her being 'bland'.

She took a couple of steps into the Throne Room, already thinking through how she could get away from this impromptu meeting as quickly as possible.

"Your brother, the King," Tineoots continued, "is out of the Palace for the day."

Syre stopped her advance on Tineoots, realising that Tineoots *wanted* something from her. She stood where she was, feeling the soft, embroidered rug beneath her feet.

She waited for what Tineoots had to say next.

"I thought it would be quite appropriate," Tineoots said, "if you might see the sense in spending the day on the throne." He broke into a yellow-teethed smile. "Keep it *warm* for him, so to speak."

Syre didn't like this at all, but she could already feel her chest tightening, believing that there might be something else coming. "Why?" she said, deciding to allow Tineoots to see her naked ignorance.

" 'Why?' " Tineoots repeated, arching his eyebrows. "Well, it has always been something of a custom that the monarch of Shellacnass, if they're indisposed, or called away for business, for one reason or another, leave behind the closest blood relative. So that any decisions that need to be made may be so made in their absence."

Syre frowned. "Isn't that why the Council of Wisemen exists—so that they can make all of the choices which'll shape Ilsnare?"

Tineoots gave a pout and held his palms open to her, as if he was somehow powerless in this matter. "I'm just telling you how things should be done, Your Majesty, with respect to the Charter of Shellacnass."

Syre found herself mouthing, the 'Charter of Shellacnass', and realised as soon as he'd done so just how idiotic—how *naïve*—she must've looked from Tineoots's perspective.

She snapped her gaze back onto Tineoots, meeting his eyes again. "And if I refuse?" she said.

"Well," Tineoots said, his eyes lolling about their sockets. "Let us put it this way—I don't think you *should* refuse. If you *refuse* then it might mean a great injustice coming to pass on Ilsnare."

Sick of all this doubletalk, Syre cut through with a sharp reprimand. "What's the reason for wanting me on the throne *today?*" she said.

Tineoots's mouth latched open for several moments as if he was admitting some sort of a defeat, as if he wanted to communicate to Syre that she had won a round in this battle of wits . . . although Syre knew—*frankly*—nothing could be further from the truth.

And, what was more, when it came to matters of governance, she couldn't care less about being left in the dark.

Finally, Tineoots spat out his reasons. "The Council of Wisemen for Ilsnare is today discussing the status of Creatures within Shellacnass."

" 'Creatures'?" Syre said, feeling her blood swill.

She was still feeling the effects of the illness one of the members of the kitchen had passed onto her. It had played havoc with her magic. While before she would get those prickling sensations running through her blood whenever she felt danger near—*or magic*—now it was difficult to be so sure.

Her ice magic seemed to prickle about her veins nearly constantly.

"Yes, ma'am," Tineoots replied, "*Creatures:* Dwarves, Elves, Fey . . . uh, and the *like.*"

"Cyclops," Syre put in, out of instinct, thinking back to the meeting of the Outcast she had witnessed at *The Soore Whip.*

"Yes, ma'am, *Cyclops* too, I daresay." Tineoots paused for a long moment here, before continuing. "It might surprise you to learn that, in actual fact, there're many different Creatures *inhabiting* the Crystal City on an illegal basis." He blinked several times and then clutched his hands together at his belt buckle. "Today, the Council of Wisemen hopes to pass a law which shall draw a line under the current *illegal* status of Creatures among the citizens of Ilsnare, allowing them—*in effect*—to become fully-fledged citizens in their own right, as you—"

Syre cocked her head to one side. "And what's the matter with that?" she said. "I don't see the trouble. The Creatures are hardly hurting anyone, are they?"

"Ah, ma'am," Tineoots continued, with a slight smile, "yes, and *no*, I'm afraid. You see, there've been reports . . ."

" 'Reports'?" Syre shot back, growing increasingly annoyed now.

In the time she'd had to think about the meeting she'd witnessed in *The Soore Whip*, she'd decided that she felt more affinity with Creatures than with most Mortals.

They shared many of the same drawbacks as the Magical did.

They had to *hide* who they truly were.

"Yes, ma'am," Tineoots went on, his tone growing a little firmer now, obviously growing impatient at having been interrupted. "To put it bluntly," Tineoots said, apparently taking a different tact, "the citizens of Ilsnare are on the *cusp* of revolting against such *foreign* influences living and working among them. And, to be quite honest, I do not think that I can blame them for one second."

Tineoots raised a finger here, to cut off any protest Syre might be in mind of launching.

"This law which the Council of Wisemen hopes to pass today will bring nothing but wrack and ruin to Ilsnare—to the *Crystal* City—and you, better than most, realise what wrack and ruin looks like."

Syre realised that Tineoots was referencing her and her brother's role in bringing down the previous Royal Family of Ilsnare.

And although she was of a mind to protest strongly, to put Tineoots back in his place, she found that she couldn't so much as raise a mumbled word.

The sickness seemed to press at her temples, almost as if it was drawing her mind tense, not allowing her to think clearly.

"So, Your Majesty," Tineoots replied, "will you be willing to veto any positive vote which the Wisemen might cast on this issue?"

It took Syre less than a second to respond. "No," she said. "No I won't."

Tineoots's features darkened. He glowered at her; showing, not for the first time, his true opinion of his monarch. "Very well," he said, and then clapped his hands together sharply.

A THREAT

Syre felt her heart sink in her chest.

She turned her attention to the doorway of the Throne Room—saw the man who trod in through it. She had never seen him before. He had a bald head, and, like Tineoots, he wore a wispy-grey robe. When he stood in the doorway, his form silhouetted by the torchlight out in the corridor, he bent down and bowed to Syre.

Despite her foggy-feeling mind, and despite the way her ice magic was prickling around her temples, she managed to find her voice. "Don't bow to me," she said.

The bald man remained in the same position for several seconds before gently straightening up. He eyed Syre as he did so.

A chill ran down Syre's spine.

She felt all her muscles clench up in her stomach.

More than anything, she wanted to get away from here.

She wanted to *get away* from Tineoots and this bald man.

Although Syre expected the bald man to continue his progress into the Throne Room, to join their conversation, he hung back, at the doorway.

It made Syre uneasy.

She slipped Tineoots a sidelong glance. "What's this about?" she said.

Tineoots smiled back at her sweetly . . . or in a way which struck Syre as *seeming* to be sweet. "I'm just ensuring that you do the right thing."

Syre shook her head, looked to Tineoots and then to the bald-headed man standing beside the doorway. "I don't know why you think you'll get anywhere with these threats of yours—like I said, I'm not going to interfere with the Council of Wisemen . . . it's nothing to do with me."

"Fine," Tineoots replied, his smile not as wide as before, but still very much present on the surface of his lips. He took a couple of steps away from the throne, toward the doorway, and the bald-headed man standing there. Just as he was about to proceed through the doorway, he turned and looked back at Syre over his shoulder. "One question," he said.

"*What?*" Syre replied, already feeling intensely annoyed by this whole episode.

"Does your brother, the King, know about your relationship with Flucknor?"

Syre felt her stomach twist completely. She balled her fingers into fists down at her side, and felt as if she might bolt forward and begin to pummel Tineoots uncontrollably. She even forgot—in that moment—that she had magic at her disposal.

Perhaps she would've tried to attack Tineoots if it hadn't been for the threatening-looking, bald-headed man.

"What're you saying?" Syre replied, taking all the energy she could muster to keep the bile out of her tone of voice . . . and, even then, she was fairly certain that she failed.

"No matter," Tineoots said with a slight smile, then turned to leave the Throne Room again.

Syre rolled her eyes, then called him back. "Wait!" she said.

Tineoots turned to her, a smarmy expression smeared all over his face now. "Princess?" he replied.

"Don't call me that," Syre said, though her voice was low now—*defeated*, almost.

Tineoots glanced to the bald-headed man, and then back to Syre. "Listen, *Princess*, and, please, pay attention to what I say."

Syre said nothing.

She hoped that her attention would be clear enough from the context.

Tineoots continued, "I have no intention of telling your brother, the King, anything about your relationship with Flucknor. And I imagine that he has perhaps guessed as much already—if Flucknor hasn't been man enough to admit it himself."

Syre felt herself seething all over, as if the blood in her veins was freezing up, forcing her into some form of action.

If only she could see things clearly—if only a blur didn't cling to everything in sight.

She wanted to get herself shot of this illness as quickly as possible.

Tineoots paused for a long—*telling*—moment. "However, I have it on personal testament that Flucknor was witnessed practising magic in the streets of Ilsnare; a crime punishable by *death* as the current law stands."

"Until this afternoon," Syre muttered under her breath, feeling her chest tighten from the mere thought of Flucknor's death.

Until now she hadn't realised how much he meant to her.

They had lived in the Palace together for over a decade now . . . they were more than lovers; they were *family*.

Despite dropping the volume of her voice to a murmur, it seemed that Tineoots heard her clearly.

"Yes," Tineoots replied, "and if he were to be witnessed practising magic—*this afternoon*—once the law has been passed allowing for greater integration of Creatures and Magical beings, then he would go scot-free." Tineoots rested his tongue on his lower lip for a long while, as if choosing his words carefully. "However," Tineoots continued, "he was witnessed to perform magic a week ago—*before* the new law came into effect."

Tineoots nodded to the bald-headed man standing beside him.

Syre glanced over the bald-headed man again, trying to absorb some other detail about him. She tried to see something in him that might strike her as familiar . . . but there was nothing so far as she could tell.

All the same, she was determined that she would remember his face for as long as she lived. She never forgot the face of someone who threatened her family—who threatened someone she *loved.*

Syre turned her attention back onto Tineoots. She shook her head. "I don't see what's in it for me," she said. "I don't see why I should veto this law the Council of Wisemen is looking to pass. What would be stopping you from handing Flucknor in?"

Tineoots gave that pout-shrug of his again. "The choice is yours, Princess, of course, I'm only giving you the options. Veto the law and I swear by my honour—by my *service*—to the Royal Family that I shall never speak a word of magic and Flucknor in the same sentence."

Despite everything—*despite the situation*—Syre believed the puffed-up passion with which Tineoots spoke of his 'honour' in service for the Royal Family.

Tineoots went on, "But if you choose to *defy* this request of mine—"

"This *threat*," she corrected him.

Tineoots inclined his head as if to acknowledge this truth. "If you choose to defy *me*, then I shall do everything in my power to see to it that Flucknor is punished to the very fullest extent of the law." He paused, met her eye for a long moment, and then added, "Do we understand one another?"

Syre's throat became drier still. Her head was swilling now. She felt as if her sinuses had all become wadded up with damp cotton. More than anything else, she wished to retreat to her quarters, to pull the silk sheets over her head and cry herself to sleep.

But she wouldn't cry.

Not now.

This wasn't a *time* for crying.

Not a time to be a *princess*.

This was a time for action.

Syre turned her attention back to Tineoots. "Okay," she replied, "I agree—just tell me what it is I have to do."

THE WATCHER WATCHED

Sheilds burrowed his hands deeply into the pockets of his cloak. The pockets themselves were lined with thick sheep's wool. He felt the warmth come back at him.

Over the past few days, Ilsnare had slipped to freezing temperatures; and he was certain, recalling his childhood fantasies, that snow was just around the corner.

The cloak had been a present in acknowledgement of his role in aiding Tineoots.

Once Sheilds had found himself to suffer from a spate of magic, at the hands of Flucknor, he'd gone directly to Tineoots—bypassing the normal channels; the ordinary means of communicating his reports.

Sheilds recalled how he'd turned up on Tineoots's doorstep and, as his childhood friend had opened the door to him, how he had smelled the rich, thick scent of roasting chicken wafting out from within.

Sheilds had felt the temptation to dip into the inside pocket of his cloak and run Tineoots through with his needle right there and then, just so that he might taste that wonderful-smelling chicken.

But he had restrained himself.

Even when Tineoots had shown him a *most-unwelcoming* expression.

And even though Sheilds had sensed that unpleasant smell of rotting eggs which inexplicably lingered on the air.

Then again, Sheilds supposed that Tineoots wasn't accustomed to finding Watchers turning up on his doorstep in the middle of the night.

Once Sheilds had revealed what he'd witnessed that day, though, Tineoots anger dissipated; and he recalled how a *most* wicked grin had begun to form on his lips as he, apparently, contemplated the significance of what Sheilds had seen; and, more likely, *who* he had seen doing it.

Tineoots had invited Sheilds in like the childhood friends they were. He had given him the very best slices of chicken flesh for his pleasure. And Sheilds had managed to get over the stench of rotten eggs from earlier.

Standing out here, just outside the main gates of Ilsnare Palace, the hood of his cloak drawn up to hide his face, Sheilds couldn't help but continue tasting the perfectly salted, succulent slices of chicken. He had savoured every last bite as if it might be his last.

He had learned, with meat, during his time at Onderswort, that it was the loftiest of privileges . . . certainly not the right which many citizens of Ilsnare seemed to believe it to be.

And it was the thought of the roast chicken which kept Sheilds warm as the winter wind whipped in through the narrow lanes and sent a shudder up his spine.

Sheilds glanced about, keeping his eye on the crowd, looking for any sign of a familiar face.

Although Tineoots's instructions had been clear; that he was to lie low here, in wait, for the time when—*if*—he was required, Sheilds couldn't help but continue his surveillance.

It'd become an automatic response for him.

Whenever he found himself within a crowd, his eyes would unconsciously switch to searching over the assembled people—looking for *something* suspicious . . . *something* to arouse a sense of interest in him.

And it was only when Sheilds glanced up, for the fourth time, to check that he wasn't being paranoid, that he noted, once more, the youthful face staring at him from the crowd. He absorbed the pale skin, and the bony body.

The miniaturised features.

A sort of *man-boy*.

Something about this boy told him that he had to be careful.

No, it told him *more* than that.

It told him that he was being *watched.*

Sheilds thought things over. He thought about when he had pursued Flucknor—and the great reward it had reaped for Tineoots.

But this was different, now.

He had been given a different task. Sheilds was to be on hand to see through the success of his previous piece of intelligence-gathering. He had to hold his ground.

What did it *really* matter that this boy was watching him?

But that didn't stop Sheilds from tracking the boy with his eyes.

As the two of them made eye contact, he watched the boy become a little hurried with his mannerisms, how he glanced about himself suspiciously; in a way which screamed to Sheilds that he had been *caught* . . .

There was an almost uncontrollable urge which bit at the pit of Sheilds's stomach.

He *so* wanted to pursue the boy.

Chase him down a backstreet.

Stick him with his knife.

Watch as the life force bled out of him onto the frozen cobblestones.

But he couldn't.

No.

This was his *new* life.

He had to remain where he was.

And so he watched the boy carefully as he left his vision.

As the boy made his way back toward the Palace.

Sheilds wondered if he should've felt something like satisfaction at being able to overcome such strong urges to pursue and kill . . . but, in truth, he felt only emptiness.

A missed opportunity.

But at least Tineoots would be pleased.

CORRUPTION AFOOT

Syre felt her temples throbbing with illness as she sat in the Throne Room and waited for the messenger to come to her from the Council of Wisemen.

That was how Tineoots had told her it would happen.

While Syre sat here, in Ilsnare Palace, seeming a *million* miles away from where anything *real* ever happened, Tineoots would register her protest against the law to be passed and a messenger would be sent asking for written confirmation.

Already, Tineoots had given her the roll of parchment declaring her opposition to the implementation of the new law, to which Syre was to press her Royal Seal.

She wondered if Flucknor *realised* just what a big favour she was doing him.

He could—*at least*—have thought to check in on her today.

To see how she was doing.

But, like always when something big was going on, it seemed, Flucknor had gone and made himself scarce. Perhaps he had ventured out of the city alongside Lou . . . maybe it had been some sort of conspiracy to leave Syre here, to rule Ilsnare, for the rest of her life.

Strangely, she wouldn't find it all that surprising.

Perhaps, at the very least, she might be able to make more headway in her search for the Webbing Armoury. But that would be just about the only positive.

Syre felt her hopes rise as she heard the *patter* of footsteps down the corridor. When she turned her attention to the doorway, to the pair of Royal Guards standing there, she heard one of them call out for the person approaching to halt and present themselves.

The answer was too hurried—too *quickly* delivered—for Syre to overhear.

But the guards were satisfied enough to allow the person through.

Her brain still feeling as if it might burst free of the confines of her skull, that the force of blood might break through bone, she took in the approaching person.

Realised that she recognised them.

Him.

It was Guilknot; Lou's personal servant.

Her eyes slipped over his bony face, and she took him in, saw that his cheeks were red from exertion.

Syre rose up off the throne then took a couple of steps toward him. Her legs seemed to move out from beneath her. She thought about retreating to the throne, but decided—having come this far—that she might not be able to make it back. "I thought you were with Lou today," she said.

Out of breath, Guilknot doubled over. When he'd got hold of himself once more, he straightened up, and looked her in the eye. "The King told me to stay behind, so that I could keep an eye on the Palace."

Syre glanced beyond Guilknot to the Royal Guards beyond. Although she couldn't be certain, she was convinced one of them was bending his head back to listen in on their conversation—no doubt in cahoots with Tineoots.

"Guards!" she called out to them, her voice feeling unfamiliarly frail; lacking in power.

As one, the pair of guards turned into the Throne Room.

"Leave us," she said.

There was a brief pause, the guards exchanged glances, and then—*finally*—the two of them acquiesced to her request.

Syre didn't speak again until she heard their footsteps become silent down the corridor.

The sound seemed to echo about her hearing, as if her skull was suddenly an echoplex.

Again, she cursed that junior member of the kitchen staff—why had they *insisted* on coming to the Palace while they were ill? It always seemed to follow that when one became sick, so did the others in the vicinity. She vaguely wondered whether Tineoots should spend less time concentrating on his power games and more on his staff management policies.

When Syre was convinced the guards were out of earshot, she allowed herself to relax a little.

Still feeling the Throne Room blur about the edges, she backed up, returned to her throne. She perched on the cushion, on the edge, feeling her whole body seized with a sudden trembling. She clutched the armrests tightly, trying to halt the effect.

As she sat on the throne, and Guilknot approached her, she reminded herself that she had to be careful. It was likely that Tineoots had spies all over the Palace. He had ears in the *unlikeliest* of places. The Eye saw *everything* . . . or so went the merchants' gossip.

Why, she might not even be able to trust Lou's humble manservant, Guilknot.

He, too, might have been compromised.

After all—*first and foremost*—he was a member of the House Staff.

And it was funny the effect that a well-placed piece of silver—or gold—could do here or there.

Syre kept her expression neutral, determined not to give anything away to Guilknot—lest of all her nausea; her *illness.* "What is it?" she said. "What've you come here to tell me?"

"Outside the Palace," Guilknot said, pointing back over his shoulder, "there's a suspicious-looking man lurking."

"Have you informed the Royal Guards?"

"Uh," Guilknot said, apparently searching for expression, before finally settling for an honest, "*No.*" He dropped his voice, kept it almost to a whisper. "Lou told me to come to you first, if he wasn't around to report in to."

"You're Lou's spy?" Syre said.

Guilknot gave a roguish smile, and a little colour entered his cheeks in a quite *boyish* manner. "Not in so many words," he said, finally.

Lou might not trust her with the location of the Webbing Armoury, but at least he trusted her so far as to allow his manservant to report in *potentially* important matters.

Syre turned her attention back to the matter at hand. "What does he look like?" she said.

Guilknot jabbed his tongue into the side of his cheek, glanced back over his shoulder once again—apparently as paranoid about being overheard as Syre was. "Quite thin, an older guy. Tanned skin. *Bald.*"

Syre thought back to the man who'd entered the Throne Room with Tineoots, and the man who'd—*ostensibly*—witnessed Flucknor performing magic in the streets of Ilsnare, and who, more importantly, was prepared to go before the Council of Wisemen with his information.

Just one more detail.

"What was he wearing?" Syre said.

Guilknot thought to himself for several moments, then said, "A thick cloak, ma'am—looked *expensive* . . . I can say that much." His voice, once more, dropped down so that it was nearly a whisper. "The way he was lurking about the market stall, I watched him there for the best part of an hour. He's gotta be in the Eye . . . he's gotta be there for a reason."

Syre thought it through for a long, silent while.

The whole room was swaying now.

It helped to squeeze the armrest of the throne as tight as she could manage . . . but it didn't mitigate the nausea completely.

She was certain that Tineoots had merely ordered that bald-headed man to keep an eye on the Palace, to make sure that she didn't try to squirm out from Tineoots's grasp . . . didn't try to skip town, get in touch with Flucknor, urge him never to return to Ilsnare.

But Syre had no intention of running.

Already, she had made her promise to Tineoots. They had struck their deal. Syre had saved Flucknor for the time being. And she had no intention of going back on her agreement.

"Ma'am?" Guilknot said.

"Hmm?" Syre said, turning back to him, already lost in her own thoughts.

"Come with me," he said. "We have to get going."

Syre felt her brain became muddled; the illness again, keeping her from being able to reason logically. Before she could get her thoughts straight once more, she felt Guilknot tug on the sleeve of her yellow-green dress.

"Come on, ma'am," he said, "there's not much time."

"I . . . I . . ." Syre just about got out, but she was never able to utter the words clearly—*so that Guilknot might understand them* . . .

As Guilknot gripped her sleeve tighter still, she felt his strength pull her up to her feet.

Feeling more unstable than ever, and, at the same time, having some dizzy thought about never having wanted to be one of those fainting—*weak*—princesses . . . she didn't want to be a princess *at all!* . . . she felt her legs give way beneath her.

With a distant, hard *thump* she fell down to the stone floor.

And lost consciousness.

A SECOND BITE
OF THE CHERRY

As **Sheilds skirted** the market stall where he was stationed, outside Ilsnare Palace, his eyes constantly on the move, attempting to pick out anything of interest, he noted the bony man-boy with the pale skin emerge from the gates of the Palace.

Something deep down in Sheilds's stomach stirred.

This didn't happen, well . . . *ever* . . .

To have two bites of the cherry—a second opportunity to recapture that which'd slipped through his fingers previously. A throat that he could *so easily* slit right open; and watch the blood pour out.

It had taken all of Sheilds's resolve to resist pursuing the man last time. It had been something of a mercy for the man-boy that he'd gone and skittered into the Palace, and so out of Sheilds's reach.

Sheilds would only be permitted past the Palace Gates with the say-so of Tineoots; and he wasn't naïve enough to think that Tineoots—no matter how *pleased* he was with Sheilds—would give him unchecked access to the Palace anytime soon.

Sheilds knew what he was.

He had made peace with it a long time ago.

And he had no intention of changing his ways.

Sheilds remained beside the market stall for another couple of beats of his heart, until, like a dog, he found the lure of the cat too irresistible; and despite all of his experience, all of his understanding of the situation with the Council, and his role in it, he simply couldn't hold himself back any longer.

Sheilds reached into the inside of his cloak, to the special compartment he had had a tailor sew into the interior lining. He felt the broad blade of the knife within; a *butcher's knife.* There would be nothing subtle about a murder with such an implement, but, in truth, Sheilds didn't have subtlety on his mind.

Only blood.

Sheilds broke away from the market stall, and he lost himself among the people; all of them dressed in their tunics and cloaks of varying colours. He was vaguely aware of their chatter, of that stuck-up Ilsnare dialect. He wondered if there might be other agents working for the Eye lurking nearby, keeping a look out for *foreigners* getting too close to the Palace; being on hand to, politely—*and curtly*—escort them away.

After all, as Tineoots had explained to him, the central purpose of the Eye's existence was, through surveillance, and other forms of protection, to assure the continuation of the values and customs of Shellacnass; and the Royal Family formed part of that.

No matter *how* they had come upon the Throne.

But those issues floated away from Sheilds's mind as he trod on through the people, knocking some of them out of his way, not bothering to pause and apologise for doing so. That would only slow him down—and give the *man-boy* a second reprieve.

And that would be unforgivable.

Sheilds, at least, would never forgive himself.

His heart beat hard in his ears as he trailed the man-boy up ahead of him. The man-boy hadn't so much as looked back over his shoulder once. He was determined, and pacing his way through the crowds, getting away from someone—or *something.*

Several times, the man-boy was too quick for Sheilds.

He seemed to have the ability of a Nymph, able to duck and weave out of sight among the crowd, almost as a subconscious quality. He supposed, like many of the servants who came to serve in the House Staff at Ilsnare Palace, this man-boy had come from a childhood on the streets of the city; and it was there that he had learned his uncanny ability to *disappear.*

But Sheilds, too, had spent time on the streets as a boy.

He knew all the tricks.

And the man-boy seemed yet to register that Sheilds was pursuing him.

Finally, the man-boy made a fatal mistake.

Just as Flucknor before him had done, the man-boy slipped down a near-deserted side alley off the main street outside the Palace. Soon enough, Sheilds was mere paces behind the man-boy. For several seconds, Sheilds walked almost on the man-boy's heels, at that deliciously *perfect* distance from his supple skin . . . and then, right when Sheilds was sure that the man-boy might make his escape, he struck.

The man-boy couldn't have seen the knife until Sheilds had brought it down on his neck for the third time.

The strokes were quick, and *brutal.*

Warm blood splashed up against Sheilds's cheeks, and he breathed in the heady—*coppery*—odour.

It was almost as if he was breathing in some brand of moonshine, taking it down deep into his lungs. And, at the same time, Sheilds felt thoroughly satisfied for what must've been the first time in weeks.

Finally . . . finally he had been able to indulge his urges.

To fulfil his purpose.

As Sheilds brought the knife down again and again, long after the man-boy had ceased moving, he heard panicked voices behind him.

But Sheilds couldn't stop himself now.

When he got himself like this, it was almost impossible for him to stop.

They would need to put him in chains first . . . or *kill* him.

Soon enough, Sheilds felt arms on him.

They tried to wrestle the knife free from his hand.

But he still managed to get in another half dozen blows before they were successful.

As they hauled Sheilds backward, away from the prostrate, man-boy's body, he felt his chest rising and falling rapidly. He felt the heels of his boots bounce up and down as they trailed over the surface of the cobblestones beneath.

All over, he realised that a layer of sweat now soaked his skin.

But, when he breathed in, he could smell nothing of the salty smell—only the bitter, metallic stench of blood.

Of the man-boy's blood.

Slowly, as they hauled him away, the little, broken body becoming further and further in the distance as a pair of cloaked figures crouched over him, Sheilds tuned himself into their words—the words of the men who held him prisoner.

". . . Lunatic . . ."

". . . Never seen anything like it . . . to think someone like that's going free . . ."

".. . Glad he works for us . . ."

".. . Wouldn't want to get on his wrong side . . ."

And then, one of the men, apparently realising that Sheilds was once more receptive to the real world . . . to the voices of other humans . . . said, "You *fool!* Just what in hell's name were you thinking? He was leading us *right there!* Taking us all the way!"

As the men bundled Sheilds around the corner, and away from the man-boy's dead body, he had sufficient conscious thought to ask, in a cool, detached voice, "Where?"

There was a moment of silence between the men hauling him along, and then the man from before said, "The Webbing Armoury."

SICKNESS

Chills ran through Syre.

All at once, her skin felt impossibly cold and insupportably hot.

The sensation shook her right down to her bones.

At the back of her throat, she tasted a bitter note of bile.

Whenever she breathed in the air of her quarters, she caught a sweet scent in her nostrils; an odour which reminded her of oranges. She could vaguely recall that a member of the House Staff had entered her quarters with a bowl of steaming-hot water . . . that had surely been what had brought the fragrance to bear on her room.

Darkness swarmed about Syre.

Sometimes it was difficult to tell if her eyes were open at all.

When she eyed the moonlight dribbling in through the balcony windows, she convinced herself that her eyes *were* open. And then she was dimly aware of her quarters, of the shapes about the room: the dressing table, the entrance leading to her en suite . . . her wardrobe.

But the world continued to constantly swirl and shift.

The sensation reminded Syre of when she had travelled with Lou by sea to Irmlesbrook. Often, during the long nights of the voyage, she would find herself alone up on the deck while Lou remained below, struck down with seasickness.

She would lean out over the side of the boat and peer into the pit-black waters while the night-time shift of sailors busied themselves with the business of keeping the ship afloat.

Sometimes, peering down into the night-time water, she wondered if she saw faces; or some kind of Creatures. Something which lay just below the surface.

She wondered if she could see something just below the surface now.

Off to the edge of her room, she was certain that she could make out figures—not much more than *shadows* . . . but she convinced herself that her mind wasn't deluding her eyes.

Three of them in all.

Three figures.

Syre clamped her eyelids shut once more. She gave her head a shake, hoping to stop her mind from showing her such delusions. But, when she opened her eyes again, the delusions remained.

And that could mean only one thing.

That what she saw wasn't a delusion after all.

Her heart rapped against her ribcage.

And the flavour of bile at the back of her throat became more pronounced.

When she breathed in the air now, she caught the scent of eggs—*rotten eggs*—and she was certain that the odour emanated from the three figures . . . all of them standing in cloaks, hidden by the shadows.

It took all of Syre's resolve to prop herself up on her elbow, and to look over the figures. She glanced back over her shoulder, feeling the world spin as she did so.

There was no one in the doorway to her quarters.

No member of the House Staff keeping an eye on her.

Syre had hardly made the observation when she heard the voice speak within her own mind.

— I sent them away.

Syre's whole body went rigid. She felt her stomach muscles clench her gut. She stared at the trio of figures, standing in the shadows. She knew, on instinct, that the voice within her mind had come from *one* of them.

Somehow, even though she hadn't heard the voice spoken aloud, she recognised the timbre and tone.

She had heard that voice before.

As she continued to stare at the figures, she noticed one of them take some steps forward. And then, as if compelled to act according to some sort of marking on the floor, the figure brought down his hood.

Syre felt a silent scream fill her throat.

Her eyes sketched over the sight.

She recognised him . . .

The horned skin.

Red skin when in a fuller light.

But a midnight blue now.

Beyond all else, Syre recognised the beady, black eyes which consumed his eye sockets. She remembered him from the meeting of the Outcast, down at *The Soore Whip.*

Syre opened her mouth to scream, but no sound would come.

She heard him—*Brotsboore*—speak into her mind again.

— I took the liberty of taking away your voice. I didn't believe that it would be constructive to our discussion.

Syre opened her mouth to reply, but, as Brotsboore had said, no sound emanated from within.

Even despite her nausea; how the whole room seemed to spin before her eyes, she managed to think through the solution.

She had to speak into his mind.

Into Brotsboore's mind.

It was an odd realisation.

But she knew it was the correct one.

Taking a pair of gulping breaths, urging her lungs to accept the air smelling of rotten eggs, she concentrated on her own thoughts—on transmitting a message into Brotsboore's mind.

She visualised the letters—strung them together into words; and then a sentence:

— *Why are you here?*

Brotsboore said nothing in reply. He merely glanced back behind him, to the pair of figures which stood at his shoulders. The two of them took a few steps forward, so that they stood alongside Brotsboore.

Brotsboore turned his attention back down onto Syre.

For a couple of seconds, Syre's attention was lost to the pair of figures standing at Brotsboore's shoulders. She thought that she had been able to make out the faces which lurked beneath the gloomy shadows cast by the hoods of their cloaks.

But as soon as she thought she'd sussed out their identities, the chain of her thoughts was abruptly broken off.

Almost as if she was attempting a transformation into a crow. As if each time she felt her body becoming weightless—*becoming lighter than air*—and she flapped her wings, she felt somebody take hold of her talons, and prevent her from taking flight.

It felt like a *cruel* trick was being played on her.

Brotsboore spoke to her again:

— *You are sick.*

Syre allowed those words to drift about her skull.

She could feel warm waves drifting through her body.

As if this declaration of her condition had brought on her symptoms all the stronger.

— *Would you like to be cured?*

Syre looked into Brotsboore's black eyes. She could see the sallow moonlight reflected in them. Her heart bucked into her throat and, for several seconds, she could hardly draw breath. She wondered if this might be some sort of a trick . . . if only she could cry out for help. She knew that Lou would make short work of these Creatures; that for whatever outward signs of fatigue he showed, he would find a renewed strength filling him if he was called into action to save her.

Like the helpless, distressed princess she truly was . . .

As Syre felt the room swill and spin about her another time, she noted Brotsboore slip a glance to the figure standing at his left shoulder. He gave the figure a firm nod.

The figure approached Syre and she realised she could make out the face which lay beneath the shadow of the cloak's hood.

She recognised this face too.

Or—should she have admitted?—the single, large *eyeball*.

The Cyclops.

She felt herself sinking back down into her silky sheets, down into the bland feather mattress. She no longer had the strength to so much as prop herself up . . . let alone to practise any of her magic.

She watched on as the Cyclops, with its—*his?*—hand reached into an inside pocket of the cloak and withdrew a glass vial. The moonlight caught the glass and gleamed over its surface. She stared upward, to the cork stuck in the top of the vial.

And then to the liquid within.

The Cyclops, as if silently prompted by Brotsboore, flicked one of his crooked fingers against the vial. The liquid within responded to this disturbance by, suddenly and—for Syre at least—without warning, shifting from its previous oily black form into a brilliant-green—*glowing*—concoction.

Syre had never much trusted potions.

She had always believed them to be the refuge of the mentally unsound.

Or else the *conman*.

As if reading her thoughts—as if anticipating her concerns—Brotsboore again spoke into her mind:

— *You have nothing to fear. This will cure your ills.*

Even if Syre had wanted to protest, there was nothing she could do. Her limbs were powerless now, struck dead with fatigue, rendered useless by the constant waves of nausea which rose up through her bloodstream.

The Cyclops reached forward and touched the rim of the glass vial to her lips.

And Syre felt the gentle chill of the glowing liquid meet her skin.

As the liquid came into contact with her tongue, she felt an odd fizzing sensation; something which reminded her of a beverage she had once been offered to try by a hobblesman: one of those many men who lumbered about the countryside, flitting from town to town, hawking their varied wares.

Once the Cyclops had tipped the rest of the vial down her throat, Syre felt the fizzing sensation occupy her cheeks. And then her blood. It passed through the entirety of her body.

As she felt the liquid taking effect, she was dimly aware of the Cyclops treading away from her, re-joining the trio of figures; taking up his place beside Brotsboore once again.

Her whole body sung with the sensation, and yet she managed to utter the words in her mind which would be transmitted to Brotsboore:

— *I'm sorry. I'm sorry for not being able to stop them. For not being able to have the law passed.*

Brotsboore gave her something like a smile.

His leathery, horny skin crinkled.

— *Not to worry. You tried your best. And, in any case, we have contingency plans. The cause is not a lost one yet.*

Feeling a gentle gasp settle on her lips, Syre managed to utter yet more words for Brotsboore to read from her mind's eye:

— *You do realise that for me, for my brother, we share your concerns. The Magical are just as desperate to be allowed into Mortal society. To not be treated as Outcast any longer.*

Brotsboore made no reply.

From the back of his throat, he made a sound approximating a gargle, and then gave her a gentle nod.

Next, he turned to the pair of figures behind him—the Cyclops, and the other figure who Syre was yet to identify—and all three of them made their way toward the window of Syre's quarters.

From deep within, Syre felt as if something might burst out through her stomach.

The potion swarmed about her body.

And she could feel an *intense* warming sensation bubble her blood.

She spoke to Brotsboore:

— *Wait! What do I do next?*

As the trio of figures approached the windows to the balcony, clearly intent on going out the same way they had—*apparently*—come in, Brotsboore glanced back over his shoulder.

Met her eyes with his own *pit-black* ones.

— *Follow your being; follow your magic. Trust and you shall fulfil your potential; and lead the whole of Ilsnare to glory.*

While Syre puzzled over Brotsboore's words, trying to bring them straight in her mind, trying to make *some* kind of sense of them, the Cyclops opened up one of the balcony windows.

A draught blew in, the winter air crisp and *sharp.*

It blew back the cloaks of the figures.

Their *hoods.*

And it was then that Syre identified the third and final figure among them.

When she saw exactly who it was.

It was a second shock that, when she tried to speak, the words came up easily from her throat, as if whatever invisible block had been present before was now removed.

"Flucknor!"

SOLITARY CONFINEMENT

Sheilds could feel a slight draught blow about his cell. It pinched his skin into pimples, and it got in down the back of the collar of his tattered tunic.

When he'd arrived here, to the gaol cell—to *solitary confinement*—he hadn't been given so much as a prison uniform. And he had already passed weeks behind bars; without anything to wash with, without fresh clothes.

Like he was back in Onderswort.

Sheilds stared at the wall, tracking the cockroach as it poked its head out of the crack in the stone blocks. As it appeared to *sniff* at the air . . . wondering whether or not it might be safe to emerge.

The sunlight made the cockroach all the more exposed whenever it did poke its head out from the shadows of the cracks in the stone blocks. Creatures such as this should've known their place, that *their* domain was the night time. They needed to show more patience, if they truly wanted to—

Sheilds snatched for the cockroach right as it wriggled about half of its body free from the crevice in the stone block. He caught hold of it by its head, and listened to it hiss to itself in his hold.

He maintained his grip on the cockroach for several seconds, enjoying looking over its black-red, segmented body in the sunrays which rippled in through the barred roof of his gaol cell.

He watched its legs writhe beneath, all of them kicking at thin air.

He had lost count of the times when he had been reduced to a situation such as this.

Back in Onderswort, when he had been found guilty of some infraction or other: sometimes for so little as stealing another prisoner's rations, he would find himself thrown by the guards into a tight gaol cell, and left to his thoughts.

In Onderswort it had been all the worse, though. There had been hardly any sunlight in the entire place to start with, but it was by the guards' insistence that the solitary confinement gaol cells featured nothing but darkness . . . that they were to be made *completely* free of any form of light.

This cell, here, in Ilsnare, was a veritable paradise in comparison.

And with a self-service buffet to boot.

As Sheilds considered the cockroach for another few beats of his heart, he thought about letting it go; about allowing it to squirm about on the dirt floor of the cell before making a break for the crevice between the stone blocks . . . to return to its cockroach life, living off the scraps of other creatures.

To be a parasite.

Like so much else of the world.

Sheilds, though, would never be a parasite.

He would never be *anybody's* to depend on, either.

That was why he had done it.

That was why he had killed the kid.

He couldn't care less that it had all but ended the Eye's hopes of finding out the location of the Webbing Armoury.

Let them *keep* their stupid power games; and he'd keep his own fancies.

Sheilds squeezed the cockroach tightly, listening to its tiny head crack between his finger and thumb. He felt the glistening, full-blooded sunlight beam down on him, giving him energy, as if it might be charging him up.

He recalled back when he had been a boy.

When that *monk* had come to his home.

His mother had been convinced—for some reason or other—that Sheilds had had fire magic in his blood. But the monk had made short work of such an investigation, concluding that Sheilds was just as flesh and blood as any other Mortal.

Sheilds wondered if his mother had been looking for some explanation; something which might contribute toward illuminating the reason why he was *how* he was.

Why, when he was a boy, did Sheilds take such joy from handing other boys beatings? From pummelling them until they were out cold?

For his poor mother, she had only been able to reconcile such a solid tug toward evil as evidence for there being magic in his veins.

She had been an ignorant woman—*kind*, but ignorant.

And there was little to gain from thinking about her.

As Sheilds chewed away at his cockroach, he gazed out through the iron bars of his cell, to the stone wall of the corridor outside. He could hear footsteps coming along the corridor. The damp *slap* which accompanied footsteps here, in the Gaol.

There was a constant layer of water lurking on the stone floors no matter what the weather did . . . and, at night, it would turn to ice; and Sheilds would be barely able to breathe for the cold.

But his decrepit heart kept on beating.

Keeping him alive.

The footsteps got louder.

Acting on instinct, Sheilds retreated back into the cell, away from the bars.

At night, he had often heard the guards entering the cells of other prisoners; handing them what he'd overheard them dub 'midnight beatings' . . . and if they intended such a beating for Sheilds—*albeit in the daylight*—then it wouldn't be without resistance.

He lurked toward the darkened end of his cell, feeling his back up against the lunky stone blocks.

There was no furniture in his cell, and he was only given one meal a day; nothing much more than a sloppy broth with a piece of soggy bread floating about in it.

Hence the foraging for cockroaches.

But Sheilds got his meal at around sundown, and there were a few hours to go before that came to pass.

When the footsteps sounded just to the side of Sheilds's cell, he felt his heart giving thick, nourishing beats, as if it might be responding to the imminent threat by calming down—by making everything happen more slowly.

He stared out at the spot, just beyond the bars, into the corridor.

Waiting for the visitor to show themselves.

The first detail which Sheilds absorbed was the wispy-grey robe. At first something told him—*almost screamed at him*—that this was a Royal Guard; come to do his best at beating him . . . to see if he could bloody Sheilds's nose.

And Sheilds was ready to show *him* just where he'd gone wrong.

However, it wasn't a Royal Guard.

Not at all.

It was Tineoots; his childhood 'friend'.

Sheilds looked over those well-manicured fingernails of his; and then the calm wrinkles about his eyes. The stout, slightly pudgy body. The pallid complexion. Ilsnare did nothing but defang a man; make him weak and *useless* for everything except city work.

In a way, Sheilds was glad that he had never fallen for such vices.

Never had the *chance* to fall for such vices.

Sheilds expected to see a pair of Royal Guards come into view; at Tineoots's shoulders.

So that Tineoots would have protection.

But they didn't come.

Sheilds had assumed, when he'd first realised that it was Tineoots, that he would be headed for the hangman's noose; that the Crystal City had decided to do that which was only *wise* with one such as himself.

To save the world from his horrors.

But it seemed somewhat unlikely that Tineoots would arrive here, to Sheilds's cell, without an armed guard if this was Sheilds's fate . . . or else Tineoots was expecting Sheilds to go quietly to the hangman's noose.

There would be a great shock to be had if *that* misconception proved truthful.

"Hello," Tineoots said, with a chubby-cheeked smile.

His eyes glittered a little in the sunlight.

Sheilds remained silent, and continued to lurk toward the back of his cell; in the shadows. He couldn't yet confirm—without a doubt—that Tineoots was alone.

That there *wasn't* a pair of guards standing just out of his vision; on either side of the cell.

Tineoots clutched his hands behind his back, as if he was simply on a late-afternoon stroll. He glanced about the cell, seeming to absorb the details; to soak up the décor so that he might later mentally critique it.

Then he shifted his glance—all his attention—back onto Sheilds.

"Good that you're not in chains, eh?" Tineoots said.

Sheilds, again, said nothing.

"That was my doing," Tineoots continued, "if it wasn't for the Council of Wisemen, you would've been given a pardon . . . on my behalf; but it's not so simple as that these days. There's none of the reverence for Royal Officials as there used to be in the past, I'm afraid."

Sheilds felt his stomach tighten. He could feel the cockroach working its way down into his digestive system. His body had become accustomed to the food of Ilsnare; it had seemed to have forgotten what it was like to live as a scavenger . . . as he had done on his way back from Onderswort; feeding off whatever he might find.

"However," Tineoots went on, "I came here today to bring you something—something which you might find useful during your stay here; before I can devise a way for you to be released."

At this point, Tineoots dug about in his robe, finally withdrawing a scrap of material from within.

He held it tight in his fist, as if second guessing himself; as if considering whether or not it *really was* something apt to give Sheilds.

For the first time in their conversation, Sheilds felt as if Tineoots deserved his attention.

Sheilds left the spot where he reclined at the back of the cell, and he approached Tineoots. As he drew closer to the bars, he glanced to the corridor, to both sides of Tineoots, and saw that Tineoots was—*indeed*—alone.

Tineoots held the bundle of fabric through the bars, and waited for Sheilds to take it from him.

Sheilds held himself still for a long few moments. He didn't want to show his eagerness at wanting to grab hold of the bundle; and yet, everything within him seemed to demand that he reach out and *take it!*

Sheilds resisted the temptation for another second before reaching out for the bundle.

As he clamped his fingers about it, he felt Tineoots resisting him. Not simply allowing the bundle to go free.

As if—*already*—Tineoots had changed his mind.

Tineoots met Sheilds's eye closely, and then watched on as Sheilds unfolded the bundle, the cloth. Within, Sheilds saw—*nestled within*—was his needle.

The sunlight had dipped in the sky, and now it twinkled down through the bars above, sending golden rays glimmering across the length of the needle.

Its sharpened tip glimmered the brightest of all.

Sheilds glanced up at Tineoots, not quite able to believe that this was really happening.

"Go on," Tineoots said, "*take it.*"

Sheilds held back for another moment before reaching for his needle, and removing it from the cloth. He felt Tineoots eyeing him closely.

Tineoots went on, "The Council of Wisemen are holding the murder weapon for evidence, so I couldn't bring that to you, unfortunately. But I can assure you that I'm doing all I possibly can to get you out of this . . . uh, *situation.*"

As Sheilds gripped the needle tightly, he felt Tineoots's eyes tracking him.

"You're valuable to us, Sheilds," Tineoots said, "and we're desperate to continue utilising you for the Eye, once this unpleasant episode has run its course."

Sheilds felt a warmth pass through him, and he glanced up at Tineoots once again. He felt the near-impossible-to-resist urge to stick Tineoots with the needle. To pierce his guts, watch him crumple to his knees, and bleed to death right before him.

As if his very being was ahead of his conscious mind, Sheilds felt, apart from himself, his hand reach out and hold the nib of the needle to the patch of skin just below Tineoots's ribcage.

Perfectly positioned so that Sheilds could thrust it upward.

Run the needle through Tineoots's heart.

Sheilds glanced up to Tineoots's eyes.

Sheilds could hear his own heartbeat in his eardrums.

He thought he heard words there, commands:

Do it. Do it. Do it!

But he resisted.

He stared deep into Tineoots's eyes, and he saw the calmness there.

He could see the solid, chilly—*cool*—resolve.

And he knew that they were one and the same.

That, despite Tineoots's outward—*soft*—appearance, that they had come from the same place, and they were headed the same way too.

Tineoots spoke to Sheilds quietly, and calmly, as if only the cloth of his robe *didn't* separate the nib of Sheilds's needle from his skin. "There will be an opportunity . . . in a few days—all I ask is that you're ready; that you stay primed, and ready to act. We'll speak again afterwards."

Tineoots made no motion to step back from the bars, to put distance between himself and the nib of Sheilds's needle. He continued to stare into Sheilds's eyes until Sheilds retracted the needle.

Slipped it into the waistband of his tattered trousers.

Tineoots smiled pleasantly then turned away.

As Sheilds listened to his retreating footsteps, he breathed in—*clear and distinct*—that same stench of rotten eggs.

But he soon put them out of his mind.

And, for the first time in days, Sheilds felt a smile breaking out over his lips.

A sincere, unrelenting warmth grip him.

Perhaps he wasn't alone in this cruel, dark world after all.

THE SICKNESS SPREADS

S yre trod about the Palace kitchens, looking for any member of the House Staff who might be present. But she couldn't find anybody. Soon enough, she gave up looking and instead turned her attention to reheating some of the beef casserole they'd had for dinner last night. She slipped the baking dish into the embering fireplace and leaned back against the cobbled-together wooden table.

The whole of the Palace was quiet these days. The illness, the one which Syre had suffered from, racked the entire population of Ilsnare.

Ever since that odd, midnight rendezvous with the trio of cloaked figures—with Brotsboore, the Cyclops . . . *Flucknor*—and the administration of the potion, Syre had been feeling much better.

Today, four nights since they'd come to visit, she was almost feeling herself.

This morning she had even attempted some basic charms in the privacy of her bedroom . . . she had left the more complicated matter of transforming into a crow for later on; for when she would eventually recover the whole of her strength.

And she *was* convinced she would recover.

Apart from the illness beyond the Palace walls, life in the Palace went on as usual.

Lou was still skulking about the Throne Room, hardly leaving; this time on the pretence of *not* catching the sickness floating about the city. But, the real reason for his unwillingness to leave his quarters, she knew, was down to the sudden death of Guilknot.

She recalled how they had held the quiet funeral service at the break of dawn, a day after Guilknot had been discovered with his throat slashed down a side alley, near the Palace. It had been soon after he'd come to Syre, demanding that she leave with him—whatever it was that he had intended.

Some days she wondered if that blade had been meant for her.

If the idea had been to have Syre outside the Palace walls so that she might be exposed.

But she had fainted before she'd got the chance.

Even today, she wore her blackest of gowns, feeling as if it was the only thing she could do for Guilknot now.

In some way—*somehow*—she felt as if she was responsible for Guilknot's death . . . it couldn't just be coincidence that his death had occurred so soon after he'd met with her.

Could it?

When she'd come around from her fainting brought on by the sickness, she'd found that the parchment with the Royal Decree was missing—that Tineoots had taken her order to the Council of Wisemen who, duly, had struck down the law which would've changed everything.

Which would've given the Creatures—not to mention herself—a new lease of life in the Crystal City.

But, as it was now, she knew from the brutal slowness with which legislation was passed, that there wouldn't come another chance like this for a decade; maybe longer. And it was all because she had wanted to save Flucknor.

To keep him for herself.

Was that so selfish?

Yes, she supposed that it was.

But, anyway, apart from that night with the trio of cloaked figures when she'd *thought* she'd caught sight of Flucknor, she hadn't seen him at all.

Wherever he was now, she hoped that he was safe.

"My *goodness*, Princess!"

Syre glanced up and saw that, as always, his footsteps silent, Tineoots had entered the room. He wore his wispy-grey robe, and he looked startlingly healthy considering the fact that, in the early-morning light, Syre would wake to the *click, click, click* of the wooden wheels of the Death Carts trundling through the streets, piling on the corpses. The bitter—*almost snarky*—call of the Collectors as they took their coins for transporting the dead to the pits well outside the City Walls.

Death, these days, had become so common—*so everyday*—that its effect had been dulled.

Although Syre could still recall her shock at Guilknot's death, she found that, after the first few servants had been reported 'gone', she had come to take this grim news in her stride.

"Isn't there *anybody* about?" Tineoots said, with a flash of his eyebrows as he strode over to her, flapping his arms as if to ward her away from the preparation of her own beef casserole.

Syre unhappily relented.

She stood back from the fireplace and watched Tineoots go about his work.

Of course, having lived an entire life of service to the Royal Household, he was much faster—*more efficient*—than her own clumsy hands were.

"Burning up, this is," Tineoots said, his voice slightly jolly.

Syre couldn't help noticing how, ever since the law to grant Creatures greater rights all throughout Ilsnare had been struck down, he had been far merrier; far more *personable* than he had been in the past.

Tineoots worked quickly to manoeuvre the baking dish from the fireplace. To do so, he used a pair of brass rods with insulated wooden handles. With the steaming object at the end of the rods, he trudged across the stone floor of the kitchens, and deposited the baking dish on the table. "There we go," he said, a smile lingering on his lips, and several spots of colour rising in his cheeks.

"Tineoots?" Syre said, taking her seat at the kitchen table, with the steaming—*delicious-smelling*—dish before her.

Tineoots wiped his hands on the sides of his robe, as if his palms had become sweaty from the simple task of retrieving the dish from the fireplace. He beamed up at her.

"What's it like out there—with the sickness?" Syre said.

Tineoots continued to smile as he replied. "Oh, *awful.* Really. Horrendous."

Syre stared down at the beef casserole, and the steam coiling up from it. She felt her heart skip a few beats. It had been a while since she'd felt the strength to handle anything as substantial as beef.

During the worst days of her sickness—before she had been administered the potion—she had hardly been able to stop the room from spinning long enough to get any sort of sustenance down.

While Tineoots dug about the drawers, searching for cutlery, sending the contents of the drawers, the silver within, clinking and clanking about, Syre spoke again.

"Have you heard any news of Flucknor?" she said.

If Tineoots was taken off guard by the question then he didn't show it. He burrowed through the current drawer, finally coming up for air clasping a handful of cutlery: spoons, forks, a knife or two. He glanced back at her. "No, ma'am, nothing at all."

The only slight clue that Tineoots might've been somewhat bothered by the question was the way that his once-beaming smile was now a mere glimmer.

Syre thought about digging for further information before deciding, in the end, that there was simply no reason to do so.

She had seen him with her own eyes.

With the Creatures.

Whatever had become of him, he had moved past her and Lou.

He had taken his own path . . . whatever that turned out to be.

"Here," Tineoots said, stepping over to the table, handing over the cutlery.

And then, with a smile curling his lips, he muttered, "Bon appétit."

NIGHT TIME IN THE GAOL

S heilds was half asleep when he heard their voices drifting along the corridor. He never truly slept—he believed this to be one of the reasons why he had managed to survive Onderswort. He never allowed himself to drift away for more than a matter of minutes. And although his cell here was more comfortable than his lodgings at Onderswort—albeit without a bed, and with nothing but soiled straw and stonework on all sides—he had remained at the same level of alertness, ready for an attack to come from any direction.

He picked out the Ilsnare accent in the voices, the way that the vowel sounds cut through the stodgier consonants. How the tone of the voice seemed to descend into a low drawl toward the end of sentences, as if the speaker had lost interest in what they were saying.

Sheilds pressed himself up into the corner of the cell, feeling the stonework against his shoulders, providing him with a much-needed point of reference. He opened one eye a sliver and peered out through the bars of his cell; already reaching inside his cloak for the needle which Tineoots had brought to him.

What his *brother* had brought to him.

Where Sheilds had grown up, on Guider Street, he had often thought about the various ebbs and flows of the people there; about how it wasn't uncommon to find that a father had created several mothers. Over the past few days, Sheilds had found himself pondering the possibility that Tineoots might well be his brother—just as Jhang was.

Such were the giddy thoughts which crept into his head while in solitary confinement, with no company save for his own thoughts . . . and, unlike Sheilds's journey here, to Ilsnare, he had had no outlet for his frustration; no way of 'letting off steam'.

Though, at least now, he had his needle.

He squeezed his needle tighter as he heard the voices creeping closer.

Although Sheilds didn't understand every word of the Ilsnare dialect, he could tell from the tone of their voices that their mood was jovial—and why not?

After all, they had their freedom.

They could walk about the city at *will*.

He listened to them approaching.

". . . You gonna go down the *Dalmer's* tonight?"

Sheilds knew that *The Dalmer's Chest* was a popular drinking hole, and one which, if he hadn't been sent away in his relative youth to Onderswort, he might well have frequented himself. Then, like Tineoots and Jhang, he might've grown his own belly . . . a *beer* belly.

". . . Nah, gotta stay in—my sis ain't feeling too sharp, and, well, you know how it is."

There was a stilted silence following this remark, and Shields knew this to be because of the sickness which was ravishing the city. He had overheard rumours from the guards; heard their personal sob stories about their parents, or children, aunts and uncles, cousins; taken from them 'too soon.'

Sheilds still found it hard to comprehend the security—the *safety*—which the citizens of Ilsnare believed was their birth rite. Then again, they had never seen a place such as Onderswort. They had never truly been to the place where hope went to die.

The guards were silent now as they stole closer to Sheilds's cell.

He felt his heart flutter up to his throat and tickle his tonsils.

He squeezed his needle all the tighter.

If he got a chance he would take it.

There would be no mistake about that.

His single, barely opened eye locked onto the bars.

He watched the guards come into view.

Their wispy-grey uniforms.

Neither of them expressing any emotion—let alone speaking.

Sheilds lurked.

And he waited.

The guards took expert care with their opening of his cell.

As one of the guards turned the key in the lock, it made hardly any sound at all.

Only a thin *click* . . . a sound which might've been just as easily made by a cockroach as it scoured the stone floor.

Searching for food.

Sheilds felt their shadows looming over him.

Blocking out the little moonlight which crept into his cell.

He grasped the needle tighter still.

And waited for them to come close.

Close enough.

Too close.

A LONG, FRUITLESS WAIT

As Syre sat on the stone wall of the stables, around the back of the night-time Palace, she couldn't unglue her eyes from the gates. She couldn't help wondering to herself—*convincing herself*—that at any given moment Flucknor would come riding on through. That he would be smiling, and that he would pull his horse up beside her and kiss her *hard* on the lips; with a thirst which she'd longed for all these days and nights.

Something which'd been lacking in her life.

"In mourning, are we still?"

Syre turned to look.

Saw that, with that same unnerving, soundless gait, Lou had emerged from the Palace.

At first, Syre was taken off guard.

He looked gaunter than ever, as if his cheeks had been hollowed out with some blunt instrument. His eyes were sunken back in their sockets, and his clothes looked somehow tatty . . . though how Tineoots might've allowed that to happen flummoxed Syre.

If there was one detail which Tineoots refused to allow to slide in those he waited on, it was the outward appearance. Then again, perhaps it was because Lou wasn't allowing anybody in through the entrance of the Throne Room.

Not even their most trusted butler.

Lou trudged up to her, and Syre noticed that he was limping slightly. It took him a couple of goes before he managed to haul himself up onto the wall beside her.

Syre felt the hearty beef casserole continue to stir about her stomach, continue to warm her blood.

For the first time in days, she felt as if she was brimming full of strength. As if she might have lung-after-lung full of air at her bidding.

When Lou finally sat up on the wall beside her, she listened to his ragged breaths. To how his breathing was shallow. Although he was smiling, she could see that the same sadness—the one which'd accompanied Guilknot's death—clung to his features. "Waiting for someone?" he said, slipping her a sidelong glance.

Syre turned her attention back to the gates.

Even now, with her brother beside her, she was convinced that she could hear the distinct sound of horse hoofs against cobblestone in the near distance.

That Flucknor was right around the corner.

She knew that she had to ask the question—that she had nothing else to lose.

"Lou?" she began, in that little sister-like manner she had perfected through the years.

"Mm?"

"It's about Flucknor," she said, and then studied Lou for any reaction. There was none which she observed.

Lou's easy smile continued to cling to his lips.

"I wanted to know something," she said.

"Go on."

Syre drew in a shaky breath, then breathed it out, feeling the exhalation just as filled with tension. "Is he involved with the Webbing Armoury?" she said. "Does he *know* where the Webbing Armoury *is?*"

Lou continued to stare at the gates leading out of the stables as if he, too, was expecting Flucknor to come riding through at any given moment. He remained very still as he considered the question, apparently deep in thought.

Finally, he gave a shake of his head.

He parted his lips as if to say something, but he made no sound.

Syre couldn't help herself adding, "You didn't trust him, did you?" She shook her head. "Not another mage—you *couldn't.* That was why you kept Guilknot close; someone without a drop of magical blood in their body, someone who you *knew* would have no use for the Webbing Armoury personally. And yet someone who you could keep close."

Lou's gaze seemed to lose focus, and Syre realised that she had spoken not a little brutally. After all, Lou must still be feeling very strongly the loss of his humble manservant. She thought that Lou would drift into silence, as he so often seemed to do whenever he sensed a battle to be fought.

But he didn't.

"I never showed him the location of the Webbing Armoury," Lou replied. "Whenever I concerned myself with matters of the Armoury, I kept him at an arm's length." He glanced back at Syre, met her eye for a long moment and then added, "The truth of the matter is that I don't trust anybody." He shook his head then stared down at the stone ground below. "I don't even trust myself."

"What'd you mean?" Syre said. "You don't know where the Webbing Armoury is either?"

But this time Lou had no intention of replying.

He simply shook his head, and then slipped down off the stone wall.

He disappeared back into the Palace, leaving Syre alone.

She turned her attention back to the gates of the stables, still convincing herself that she could hear the *clop* of horse's hoofs on the cobblestones outside.

And that Flucknor, at any given moment, would return.

REUNITED

As Sheilds stole out of the Gaols, pleasantly surprised to find that he was met with no resistance; he thought again about those guards he had killed back in his cell.

It had been so easy.

Neither of them had had time to shout out.

The swords they'd held in their hands had done them no good whatsoever.

Sheilds had slipped his needle through the throat of one guard; could still hear those husky, whispered screams echoing about his head.

He had jabbed the other up through his ribcage, piercing his heart.

The two of them had fallen at his feet.

As Sheilds pressed himself up along the stone wall of the Gaols, he felt the warm dampness on the front of his tunic; and he knew that it was from one—or *both*—of the guard's blood. Although Sheilds had acted quickly, realising that time was of the essence after what he had done, he had ended up being *rinsed* with their blood as it had spurted free from its mortal flask.

Sheilds listened carefully, expecting all manner of things to greet him up ahead; for a whole group of guards to be awaiting him; anticipating his escape.

The fact of the matter was, although Sheilds had felt something of a shifting in his attitude toward Tineoots—that he had even come to consider him as something like a brother—he could never allow his sense of suspicion to drop.

Not even for a second.

From his time in Onderswort, he knew that the only true *suckers* were those who allowed themselves to *trust* . . . those were the ones who would wake, in the middle of the night, their screams spluttering with blood; and their arms desperately scrabbling for the foe who had long since departed . . . who had long since been proclaimed the victor of that particular life-death struggle.

When Sheilds reached the guard post of the gaol, he noted the half-asleep guard at the desk.

Although there was really no need to kill the man—*young*, and, in a way, reminding him of the man-boy he had killed, Sheilds really couldn't resist.

The man hardly made a sound as Sheilds first eased his needle into the man's chest, and then eased the man down onto the stone floor, underneath the wooden desk and out of sight to the cursory glance.

Sheilds dressed himself in the man's wispy-grey uniform and then used the keys to let himself out through the succession of iron-barred doors.

Finally, less than five minutes since he had first smelled blood, Sheilds found himself out in the winter's night.

Outside the Gaols.

A free man once again.

He glanced about the street and, sure enough, he spotted a carriage, drawn by two horses, awaiting him. He turned his attention onto the orange glow of the lamps which hung from each side of the carriage. And he looked up to the elderly, decrepit driver sat up on the mount.

The driver's silver-blue hair, and his long, wiry beard somehow brought Onderswort back to mind. As he crossed the cobbled street, and approached the door to the carriage, he wondered what it was exactly which tickled his memory. It wasn't until the door to the carriage opened from within, and Tineoots smiled out from inside; not until Sheilds allowed himself to sink down into the soft, *sprung* seat of the carriage, that he finally grasped just what this was.

The driver, he was just like the one who had carted him to Onderswort.

All those years ago.

Impossible, of course; that man—the *driver*—would be long-since dead.

And, in any case, he had greeted Sheilds, and the other prisoners, on another land mass entirely. As far as Sheilds understood, the driver had never come to Ilsnare.

Outside, Sheilds heard the *snap* of reins coming down across the backs of the horses.

The carriage jerked to life.

"What's the matter?" Tineoots said, from out of the darkness. "You look as if you've seen a ghost."

Sheilds had to admit, at least to his mind, that he had.

A DECISION MADE;
A LOAD CAST OFF

J ust as during the previous night, Syre found herself restless. She twisted and turned beneath her bedsheets, unable to keep herself from knotting her silky nightgown. For some reason, she hoped that Flucknor would come to her in the night, that he would drift out of the shadows, and *be* with her here.

So that she wouldn't feel so alone.

She could hardly think a thought without finding herself becoming lost down a never-ending, rabbit warren of side-roads, dead-end-lanes and ever-circling streets. It reminded her of the labyrinthine series of passageways which led up to the Palace, and which were intended to make a foot-assault on the Palace near enough impossible.

Did the architect of such a masterstroke ever consider how they might present an opposite problem to anyone who hoped to flee the Palace?

How one who didn't intimately know the streets surrounding might easily become as directionless, and under assault, as the invaders?

When Syre opened her eyes, she saw the moonlight coming streaming in through the balcony windows. A full moon. She knew she wouldn't have a hope of finding any sleep.

Mind made up, she shucked her bedsheets and clambered over the floor of her bedroom, and then to the balcony windows. She pressed her forehead up against the glass and peered out onto the balcony. She half expected to see Flucknor there, lurking nearby, him wanting to be close to her as much as Syre wanted to be close to him.

But, of course, he wasn't there.

She looked over the Palace Gardens, expecting to find something to steal away her attention, but there was nothing. Only a pair of guards striding back and forth, patrolling the various animals sculpted out of the thick bushes.

She remained at the window for another couple of moments before deciding that, if Flucknor wouldn't come to her then she would go to him.

She was tired of his lies—tired of him doing his level best to hide out from her; and to conceal the more unpleasant aspects of Ilsnare.

She knew what went on.

She knew *all about* the unpleasantness.

So attempting to hide it was a truly dim-witted task.

Syre picked out a black outfit; a pair of riding trousers, and a baggy tunic which'd once belonged to Lou. She found that men's clothes were often more durable on nights such as this one, with the snow threatening to fall. Women's clothes were only made for looks.

Dressed, Syre glanced about her quarters, wondering if she should bring something else along with her. The funny thing was that, because she hadn't been out of the Palace for a good few weeks—owing to the sickness—she felt as if it was some *great* event.

As if it wasn't something which she'd constantly done in the past without so much as a second thought.

She had to *tell* herself not to give the matter a second thought now.

Or maybe—*just maybe*—it'd be better to stay in tonight.

Perhaps Flucknor *would* return . . . albeit in the company of that trio of men in cloaks.

She sat back down on the edge of the bed. Suddenly she felt drowsy. The thought of sprawling herself out on the soft mattress, of bringing the sheet over her head until morning—until the snow had fallen—seemed all the more attractive than venturing out in the soon-to-be falling snow.

And with her having just got over the sickness . . . she didn't want to get herself ill again.

She hadn't exactly had the opportunity to grill that trio of cloaked figures who'd entered her room on the intricacies of their potion—of just *how* it functioned.

No, perhaps it *was* better to rest.

She would see more in the day, in any case.

In the daylight everything would be clearer.

Mind made up, she shucked Lou's thick sheepskin cloak and lay back on the bed, staring up at the ceiling. Feeling as if each of her eyelids weighed a ton.

OUTSIDE ILSNARE PALACE

"Here, take this," Tineoots said.

Sheilds turned his attention to Tineoots, and he examined the vial he held out to him. He scowled at the glass. It was an oily-black colour. It seemed thick and gloopy. "What is it?" Sheilds said.

Tineoots shrugged. "It'll keep you from getting the sickness."

Sheilds raised his eyes to Tineoots. "A potion?" he said.

"Uh-huh," Tineoots replied, "if you like." He handed the vial over to Sheilds. "Just knock it back, okay?" Without warning, Tineoots broke into a wide, toothy smile. "If you want to *live*, that is . . ."

Sheilds held the glass vial in his fist, feeling the cool quality of the glass up against his skin. He glanced out of the carriage window, seeing Ilsnare Palace growing up out of the gloomy night.

Looking at the sky, the frumpy clouds, he could tell that it was going to snow later on. He'd learned to recognise the signs back at Onderswort—back when he'd been working out in the fields. Back then snow had meant great joy among the inmates. It'd meant that they would be allowed inside their bunkhouses, to lie themselves down on the floor beside the rickety, old wood-burning stove. And, most often, they wouldn't need to return to work the next day; or the *next* if they were really lucky.

Now, though, the snow was nothing but a nuisance.

For what Sheilds had in mind for this evening, at the very least.

As Tineoots had explained on the way here, on the way to the Palace, he had attempted to kill Syre with the sickness—by having an infected member of the House Staff be in the kitchen at the same time as Syre.

And he *had* succeeded in infecting her.

However, she seemed to have pulled off a miraculous recovery. So he had opted for a far more direct route this time around . . . it was Sheilds's task to kill the princess in her bed.

Why Tineoots wanted Princess Syre Dorf dead was a mystery to Sheilds, but he didn't think to probe the matter any further. He was a humble assassin. He would stick to what he did best—what he had proven, over and over again, to be something above and beyond a mere interest—and he would snuff out the princess once and for all.

Tineoots had made Sheilds all sorts of assurances, all sorts of promises which involved a lordship, and lands to spare. But Sheilds, in all honesty, would've done the deed for no pay whatsoever. He took pride in his work; and he needed no recompense to feel satisfaction.

Tineoots had been glad to note that Sheilds had had the presence of mind to suit himself up in one of the guard's uniforms from the Gaols. He would look just like any other Royal Guard once he had entered the Palace; and would be able to go undetected for the requisite time that was required.

Sheilds turned his attention back to the vial again. He slipped his thumb up against the cork, and squeezed it free from the neck. He gave the vial a slight shake.

At once, the oily-black colour was replaced by a brilliant-green glow.

Sheilds glanced once more to Tineoots, who was smiling from ear to ear, and then he knocked the potion back. He felt it fizzle about the inside of his mouth; and it seemed to give him just the kick he required.

"Good luck," Tineoots said, and then opened the carriage door for him.

Sheilds stepped out onto the cobblestones.

As Sheilds approached the doors around the back of the Palace, the doors which led to the stables, he felt the falling snowflakes brush against his cheeks.

A couple of times, a fierce wind blew and he was forced to pull up the collar of his uniform to guard against the chill.

When he got to the stable doors, he reached down into the pocket of his guard's uniform and removed the skeleton key which Tineoots had given him.

He fit the key to the lock.

When he twisted it, he could feel the rusted-up mechanism give a sight *groan*.

Creaking hinges and rusted locks seemed somewhat out of keeping for a Palace, but, then again, he supposed that the House Staff had been somewhat light ever since the sickness had hit Ilsnare.

He shot a cursory glance up onto the ramparts.

But there were no Royal Guards in sight.

Tineoots had made sure of that.

Sheilds slipped in through the gate then brought it shut behind him.

He walked across the iced-over cobblestones of the stables, already catching the strong stink of horse flesh and leather.

He had always hated horses.

He supposed his hatred had taken on fresh life during his time at Onderswort.

He could still recall how the Mounted Guards would march from side to side on the backs of their horses, their long rat's tail whips dangling from their fingertips. The Mounted Guards were always ready to bring down their whips across the shoulders of any inmate who—in their humble opinion—was not pulling their weight in the fields.

Although Sheilds was sure that nobody was watching the stables, he walked quickly, and felt inside his guard's uniform for the needle. When he eventually located it, he felt the nib poke into his palm. There was a slightly warm sensation and he felt a drop of blood slide down his skin.

He caught that coppery scent in the air.

When he reached the door which led from the stables into the Palace itself, Sheilds stopped, pressed his back up against the stone wall of the Palace, and then he licked off the droplet of blood which'd run down his palm.

It sent a thrill through him like nothing else.

Almost, he considered, like holding up a bloody rag to a hunting hound's nose and then watching it dash off into the distance.

To make the kill.

Sheilds shifted in through the doorway of the Palace, and out of the freezing-cold night.

He hoped, when he got through with this, that the snow wouldn't yet have fallen.

FOOTSTEPS

Syre had been drifting in and out of sleep for several minutes when she became aware of the footsteps outside her quarters. To begin with, as she felt herself slipping off into the world of dreams, she thought that it might only be happening within her imagination.

Finally, though, when she came to the conclusion that it was *very much* happening, she shifted her weight forward. She lay on her side, beneath the bedsheets, and stared out into the darkness of her bedroom; to the doorway which led to the corridors outside.

Her heart hung in her throat, and she felt all her muscles lock tight.

Over the course of the past few minutes, she felt as if the air temperature had plummeted several degrees. Outside her window, she could see that the snow was falling in drifts. By morning, when she looked out through her window, to the stables, the cobblestones would be layered with snow.

She held herself still, almost certain that she was being watched now. She knew she had to take care.

That, due to the sickness, the House Staff was in short supply; and it would be easy for someone wishing her ill will to make it to her quarters if they were particularly stubborn . . . if they managed to outfox the Royal Guards posted in strategic points about the corridors.

As Syre's eyes shrugged off the grogginess of sleep, they grew more and more accustomed to the surrounding darkness. And to the form of the gloom.

And she was certain—*certain*—that somebody was out there.

Waiting for her.

Creeping closer.

All the time.

CLOSING ON THE KILL

Sheilds crept on through the stone corridors already feeling a smile sneak its way onto his lips. He had his needle drawn down at his side now, and he could feel his heart giving a simple and steady series of *throbs* as he paced his way along.

This would be—by far—the most daring of his murders.

Perhaps it would stand the test of time; be written about in history books.

The murder of Princess Syre Dorf of the Kingdom of Shellacnass.

He recalled his time as a child, back in school, hearing about all the daring assassinations of royalty down the years. Somehow Sheilds had always felt a certain affinity with those types.

With the *assassins* . . . despite the teacher's attempts to strike an appalled tone.

And now was his chance to truly join their ranks.

He glanced into her quarters.

He could see her form, in bed, slumped up beneath the bedsheets.

This would be so quiet—*so subtle*—and there was nothing that anybody would be able to do to stop him now. It didn't matter that Tineoots had accounted for an escape plan for

Sheilds; that he would find his way out of the Palace if he only followed instructions.

This moment, right here—*right now*—was the pinnacle of his life.

As Sheilds took the final steps into the bedroom, the needle down by his side, he could still taste the coppery flavour of his own blood in his mouth, and he knew that, in a few moments' time, there would be blood *all over the place!*

He eyed the sleeping form, brought the needle up in his grasp, and took one more step.

It was then that he felt something resisting him.

Something *holding* him back.

At first Sheilds was eminently confused.

He tried to manoeuvre himself around.

To take a look at what restrained him.

But he couldn't shift off his spot.

It was right then that Sheilds felt something solid strike him over the head.

For a long second, he grasped his needle as tightly as he could and swiped at the air . . . aware all the time the gesture would do no good.

He crumpled down onto the stone floor of Syre Dorf's quarters.

And felt the darkness seep in.

CAPTURE

Syre felt her breathing coming shallow.

Every step she took seemed to sap her of energy.

Her heart beat down in her stomach.

And she could feel ice magic prickle in her veins.

She glanced back over her shoulder, to her quarters.

She could just about make out the glow of moonlight through the doorway.

She snatched another breath, determined to get clear of the scene.

When she was back down in the kitchen she would have time to think.

Some time to *process* just what had happened.

Suddenly, without any sort of conscious thought, she stopped dead.

Up ahead of her, in the corridor, she noticed another form in the darkness. Before she had a chance to stop herself, she found herself saying, "Flucknor?"

"It's me," Lou replied, and took a couple of steps forward so Syre could make out his features.

Syre's heart sunk a little to see that it was her brother.

"What happened?" Lou said.

Syre felt the words stripped off her tongue.

She heard stirring over her shoulder.

She could hear them coming.

Dragging the would-be assassin between them.

Someone—*it had to be Lou*—lit a nearby torch. Slick orange light flooded the corridor. It licked at the walls, and pressed the shadows back into the corners.

Syre turned her attention onto those coming toward them.

And then—*finally*—she could make them out.

Sully; or as he was otherwise known: Sulliman, Royal Protector of the Plains.

And then there was Rut; or: Rutterness, Royal Guardian of the Waterways.

She took in Sully first, and his neck-long black hair; his *black* eyes. And his wiry body.

Then she looked to Rut, almost an opposite impression; blond, and with a round, cuddly figure.

Between them, they held the would-be assassin.

She took in his bald head, and how he wore the uniform of the Royal Guards. That was, without question, how he had been able to get so far through the Palace.

And if it hadn't been for Sully and Rut she would be dead right now.

Although Syre knew—*logically*—that she should be delighted to find herself among the company of such great friends, she couldn't help but feel a tingle of anticipation.

It had all happened so quickly.

As Syre had been lying in bed, she'd made sense of those shadows coming out of the gloom, and then, as they had sneaked closer, she had heard the familiar voices.

The voices had been held to a hurried whisper, telling her to get out of bed from the other side.

To *trust* them.

And despite everything that Syre had gone through with Sully and Rut, she had paused for a long while . . . unable to do what they demanded of her.

Now, though, she could see things more clearly.

That they had *intercepted* this man.

Syre turned away from the scene, still unable to smile. She looked to Lou, feeling as if he was the one to blame here. "Why didn't you tell me Sully and Rut were back?" she said.

Lou met her eye for a second, before turning his attention downward to the intercepted assassin at their feet. "I didn't want to worry you," he said, "but the fact is that I've been worried about something like this for a long time."

"But, why?" Syre found herself saying. "If they wanted the throne then why didn't they go after you?"

A slight smile caught at the corner of Lou's mouth. "No," he said, "they're still afraid of me—afraid that I'm still in possession of the Webbing Armoury; that I'll be able to strike down any threat. But, at the same time, they know that I have no one close to me—and hence I have no heirs." He turned to face Syre, the smile disintegrating. "By killing you now it would remove another obstacle. Something they won't have to worry about later on, when I die."

Syre felt her breath hitch in her throat. "*Die?*" she said. "Why'd you think you're going to die?"

Lou shrugged. "Sometime it'll happen; either when I'm an old man, or some discontented citizen . . . it's *inevitable*," he added, turning back to her and feeding her a searing gaze.

Syre was lost for words for another few beats of her heart, when she turned her attention back to Sully and Rut. It was only now, with the slightly surreal sight of the would-be assassin between them, that she managed a smile. "It's great to see you two," she said, "and thank you for saving my life . . . probably not for the first time."

Sully and Rut smiled back at her.

The would-be assassin they held together stirred in their grasp.

Apparently coming around from his daze.

The would-be assassin jerked suddenly in Sully and Rut's hold, but they kept a tight grip on him.

He couldn't extricate himself from their hold, but he could tilt his head upward, so that he might look at Syre.

And Syre stared back at him.

Before she could think it herself, she heard Lou's voice. "Recognise him?" he said.

Syre remained quiet for several moments, waiting until the point when she was certain Lou was going to rush her for some sort of answer. And then she spoke.

"Tineoots," she said, turning back to Lou, "he was the one who let him into the Palace—it was Tineoots who wanted me dead. This man is an associate of his."

Lou nodded to himself.

Of course Syre had said nothing about how Tineoots had blackmailed her into interfering in the Council of Wisemen's attempt to pass a law affording Creatures greater rights throughout Ilsnare.

And it had seemed, on the surface, that Lou had accepted her intervention without so much as a word of criticism . . . she had said something along the lines of curtailing 'discontentment' among the citizens of Ilsnare.

Now, though, she could see the pieces of the puzzle slipping into place within Lou's mind. All that might remain for Lou to work out was exactly *how* Tineoots had managed to blackmail her—what sort of leverage he had used against her.

When Syre glanced back over her shoulder, she noted that a pair of Royal Guards had materialised out of nowhere. Lou gave them a nod, entrusting them to the care of the would-be assassin, relieving Sully and Rut.

The four of them stood and watched the Royal Guards lead the would-be assassin away.

Once they'd slipped from sight, Rut sparked up, grasping something in his fist. "This is the weapon," he said, showing them a large, thin metal pike. "When he first came around he spoke of it as his 'needle'. *My needle, needle, where's my needle?*" Rut said in a mockingly humorous tone, but it failed to raise so much as a chuckle in the others.

Lou remained staring at the weapon for a long few moments, before he broke the tension between them with a clap of his hands.

When Syre read Lou's expression, she was surprised to note that he was smiling.

It must've been the first time she'd seen him smiling in *months*.

"You two fancy a drink after your hard night's work?"

After thanking Sully and Rut again—giving each of them a welcome hug—she slipped away from the group, telling them that she'd catch up with them later.

Perhaps tomorrow.

That she was feeling a touch tired.

She *was* still getting over the illness, after all.

And, just like that, they left her alone.

Lou assured her that a pair of Royal Guards would be briefed on the night's occurrence and be instructed to be especially vigilant for the remainder of the night. He would post extra guards about the ramparts, too . . . in all the chokepoints which surrounded her quarters. He gave her another reassuring smile; and she couldn't help thinking that Lou had got just what he'd wanted . . . that— *somehow*—he *had* seen this coming all along.

Tonight was just the culmination.

And now he would celebrate.

Did that make her simply bait in his trap?

Syre thought on this as she listened to Lou, Sully and Rut's voices drift away down the corridor. She returned to her quarters, stared out through her balcony windows, and saw that the snow was falling in flurries now.

Tomorrow the whole of Ilsnare would be covered.

And all those dark things—the types of things which concealed themselves in the night—would no longer have any place to hide.

She would no longer have any place to hide . . .

BIRD'S-EYE VIEW

S yre felt the freezing air beneath her wings.

This was the first time she had taken flight since her sickness.

She had been worried when she'd pushed back the balcony doors, stepped out onto the precarious stone ledge. But she hadn't been worried about falling. She knew the truth, that everybody—at one time or another—would have to die.

No, she had been more frightened that her magic might've deserted her, that she might've—*somehow*—lost the ability to transform herself into a crow.

But that fear had turned out to be ill-founded.

Because, here she was, flapping her way across the rooftops of the Crystal City, the snow coming down all around her, and her tiny, bird's body shivering with the cold.

Normally, when she snuck out of the Palace in the dead of night, she would transform into a crow only for the duration of the journey from her balcony to the walls outside.

Tonight, however, she had decided that she would take a longer flight.

That she had rested—*recuperated*—for time enough.

She wished to stretch her abilities . . . see if she had the nous to pass a *proper* test.

Although Syre had taken to the air more times than she could count, ever since she bewitched herself to the body of a crow, she found herself each time surprised at the details she noticed at seeing Ilsnare from above.

The glass rooftops, by now, of course, were dusted with snow crystals. The few of them which had lights lit up within seemed almost like welcoming beacons. She could almost imagine herself landing on those roofs and, in crow form, somehow stealing her way inside.

She thought about appearing within the warm buildings.

But she knew she'd never be welcomed here.

That she would always be an Outcast; for one reason or another.

And that was why she was headed for *The Soore Whip* in search of answers.

Where else might she think to look for Flucknor?

And now that her strength was restored, she knew it was as likely a place as any.

With her beady crow's eyes, the eyes which focussed far sharper than her own—*Mortal*—eyes might comprehend, she took in the side alley which ran behind *The Soore Whip*. She had arrived to that back alley for the first time after overhearing that older woman at a market—someone who'd either been a Creature in disguise; perhaps extremely able at transforming into a human; or else a Mortal sympathiser for the Creatures' plight.

This time, though, she had no assurances that there would be so much as a single Creature present in the tavern.

She was certain that the Creatures changed locale constantly to avoid being surveilled by the Eye.

As Syre settled herself down in the back alley, she felt as if it was more than simply a wild shot. She noted that the snow weighed down everything, that it was layered so thick that—even as she transformed back into human form—she felt her boots sink into the cold, white stuff.

She looked to the back door, more hopeful than anything else.

And, taking a deep, though halting, breath, she reached out and pounded her fist against it.

Syre soon lost count of how many heartbeats had struck her throat. All she knew was that she'd been waiting longer than she could comprehend. With each passing second, she was convinced that she heard some giveaway sound from within; a cough, the *scuff* of a boot sole against the inside floor. But, in the end, she had to come to terms with the fact that there was no response at all . . . and what was she *thinking?*

It was already late.

Later than any public house in Ilsnare had a licence for.

And she couldn't help thinking that the pub landlord, know-ingly hosting a meeting of the Outcast in some back room, would take extra-special care not to arouse the suspicion of any passing Royal Guards . . . let alone those who lurked about in the crowds:

The Watchers.

She stepped back from the doorway, already wondering if she still had enough energy for another transformation. Perhaps she would walk her way back to the Palace and save her energy to fly back over the walls.

However, as she turned her back on the doorway to *The Soore Whip*, she heard an unoiled *creak* of hinges up above her head.

She turned to look.

And saw the figure peering out through an upper-floor window.

It was Flucknor.

THE SOORE WHIP

The warmth within *The Soore Whip* was almost unbearable at first. Syre only realised how cold her cheeks had got when she reached up and laid her palms against her skin. She supposed that her transformation into a crow hadn't gone anyway to protecting her from the elements.

With Flucknor taking a steady hold of her arm, he helped her into a cosy chair by the fireplace which still had a few pieces of flimsy kindling burning.

The whole of the pub had been shuttered hours before, and the stools were all upturned on the table tops, apparently so that the proprietor could wash the floors. She caught a strong scent of soap suds on the air; mixed in with the bitter and—*to Syre at least*—greatly unpleasant odour of hops.

Syre sank down into the cushions of the armchair, and watched on a little distantly as Flucknor set about hoiking the boots off her feet, and then—her feet bare—propping them up on a wooden footstool.

Syre felt the prickle of the ice magic within her veins protesting against the overbearing warmth, and—no doubt—wishing to sweep her away just as fast as possible.

But she held herself still.

She knew the importance of 'walking in weakness'—she needed to learn to control the adverse effects of the sun and fire on her ice magic . . . otherwise, if she was to merely *indulge* her ice magic, it would only tempt it to seize control of her.

One of the reasons why Lou had shut away the Webbing Armoury—the Webbing Blade, Bow and Cloak—was because he was afraid of his ice magic taking hold of him.

Of pummelling him down into a deep pit from which he had no chance of escaping.

It had happened to mages before—and frequently—through the ages.

Syre knew the logic to it . . . she *understood* why she couldn't allow her own magic to overwhelm her. It would be too much for her Mortal soul to bear.

Before Syre had had the chance to say anything meaningful to Flucknor, he handed her over a bowl of steaming chicken broth; a wooden spoon so that she might serve herself, and a pair of warmed-up, well-buttered bread rolls.

Syre took this all with great appreciation.

She hardly had the strength to smile a 'thank-you' before delving into her broth.

At first, she spluttered a little on her soup, but then it went down more easily.

The sensation of the chicken soup slipping down her throat, warming her from the chest outwards, was overwhelming following the chilly journey here.

She felt it swill about her gut.

As Syre ate in the silence of the deserted, darkened pub, she found herself glancing about, to her surroundings.

The Soore Whip featured many stuffed animal heads on the walls; bulls, horses, wolves, and others. There were also many weapons, perhaps the very ones which were used to make the kills. It gave Syre a slightly creepy feeling in her gut. She had never enjoyed hunting animals for sport, although she knew many men did. She recalled when Lou had first become King of Shellacnass and had been visited by the King of Rozark, from the neighbouring kingdom. Lou had been forced, out of courtesy, to put on some sort of *royal* entertainment for his guest; to take the King of Rozark out to the Hunting Grounds.

Syre finished up the soup and handed her bowl back to Flucknor. "Thank you," she managed to vocalise this time.

Flucknor took the bowl from her with a nod, and slipped away.

For a couple of moments, Syre was alone in the room.

Looking about the place, to the many wooden tables stained with ale, and the walls covered with pockmarked stains, she wondered just why men were so inexplicably drawn to such places.

To her it seemed a place of great misery; where the menfolk of the city came along to 'drown their sorrows', as she'd heard them say.

She thought back to her childhood, to when she had grown up in Endmere.

It had been much the same in her village; at the town pub: *The Mocker's Pit.*

It had burned down, like everything else, in the fire.

She could still recall how she and Lou had escaped through the delivery tunnel in the basement of the pub, and out onto the plains.

Many hadn't managed to escape.

Her mother and father . . .

When Flucknor returned to the pub, she saw that he had several others with him.

At first, Syre believed that it was the two from before, from her quarters; that it was Brotsboore and the Cyclops. But there were more of them now. Although it was tricky with the dim light in the pub to distinguish all the figures clearly, she was almost convinced that there were five of them in all; Flucknor included.

None of them wore cloaks, tonight.

And that told her that they found the pub to be safe.

Safe to show themselves in their true forms.

Syre's focus turned onto Flucknor once more, but, before she could speak, he spoke to her. "Once you've heard what I have to say, you're going to have to leave," he said.

Syre felt her chest tighten.

Ice prickled her veins.

She looked to the other figures looming at Flucknor's shoulders, now feeling very far from being welcome. She realised that the broth hadn't served as a hearty welcome, but more of a matter-of-fact remedy for one who'd been outside on a bitterly cold night like this.

Even as she turned her attention back to Flucknor, she couldn't quite believe that he was speaking to her like this, in this tone. They had been lovers; he had been the closest she'd ever allowed any person to her.

And now he was tossing her away.

As if she was nothing more than a mongrel pup.

But the transformation, the flight of her crow, had taken the wind out of her sails, and she wasn't in any sort of mood for an argument.

Flucknor nodded to the others behind him. "I believe you've met Brotsboore, and Rintersyart."

Syre glanced in the direction of the Cyclops, realising that his name was Rintersyart.

Flucknor continued, "And another, who I don't believe you have met, is the owner of *The Soore Whip*, Fhan."

Syre watched on as a squat, round, cannonball of a man lumbered into view.

He wore a tunic which exposed a sliver of his feather-white stomach.

His trousers only just brushed his ankles.

And he was bare-footed.

He gave Syre a stout nod and a grunt by way of greeting.

Syre supposed that pub landlords were unaccustomed to dealing with females.

Or, for that matter, anybody with a degree of cleanliness or manners.

It felt as if these forms in the dark were suddenly threatening; that they might bear her ill will.

"What we stand for," Flucknor said, "is nothing less than equality among all—throughout not just Ilsnare, although Ilsnare is a start, but through all of the Kingdom of Shellacnass . . . and then, once we've achieved that, through the *entire* world."

Syre felt her eyes bobbing about their sockets, wandering over the Creatures; over Brotsboore's horned, rash-red skin; and then to Rintersyart—*the Cyclops's*—single, enlarged eye at the centre of his face.

"And I must tell you this now," Flucknor said. "We will not abide by governors, whoever they might be."

Syre again felt her chest tightening.

Her heart hammered against her throat.

Then Flucknor finished. "Unless they are willing to work *with* us."

More than anything else, Syre wanted to cry out in protest, to shout out to him that she felt this so strongly—that all should be equal—that she saw no reason for his unkind words; for the way in which he was attempting to push her out . . . to push her *away*.

It was Brotsboore who spoke up next. "We cannot tolerate those who actively work against our demands; those who do all in their power to keep us from our state of freedom; those who keep us to the frontiers meaning that we become the Outcast." He paused for a long moment and then added, "Mortals, Creatures, Magical beings, we should all live together in this world in peace . . . there is no other way."

Syre turned her attention back to Flucknor, now finding her voice. "Fluck," she said, "please, you have to understand that I didn't want to do anything to interfere with the Council of Wise-men's law; and all I wanted was for you—*us*—to be safe." And then she added, "I made a deal, with Tineoots . . . he wanted to strike down the law, before it had a chance to come to pass. He forced me into a signing a Royal Decree which would stop it being passed, he threatened me; told me that you would suffer, for illegally practis-ing magic in the streets of Ilsnare, if I refused."

The pub, all of a sudden, slipped into silence.

She wondered how much of this Flucknor had already heard.

How much he had already understood.

And then Flucknor finally replied, "Whatever the circumstances, there is no way back now—not for me. I am too far invested in the cause. In *our* cause."

Syre glanced desperately about the faces of the others, as if im-ploring them to come to her aid, for them to offer to give Flucknor a sprinkling of reason . . . to demand that he *be* reasonable.

But nobody said anything.

Flucknor spoke for the last time. "Blackmail is an ugly thing," he said, "but sometimes—*on this occasion*—it was the only way of making our needs felt." He sniffed a couple of times, glanced back at Brotsboore for no more than a second then turned to Syre. "The only way that we could make the Council of Wisemen understand was with the sickness, the one which we spread about the city . . . even that, though, even though we have decimated Mortal families, even though we have brought illness to bear on innocent lives, hasn't been enough to assure what is truly right for all." He shook his head. "No, Syre," he said, "it's best that you forget about me—about *all* of us; and that you be on your guard."

Syre couldn't quite believe what she was hearing.

This was *Flucknor*, the one who'd she'd always thought to be so reasonable. He had never spoken like this with her before; and whenever she had mentioned such things, whenever she had broached such topics, he had been quick with a riposte.

Feeling as if she was being scrutinised under their group gaze, Syre rose up off the armchair by the fireplace, and then shifted past them all; headed toward the back door.

As she stepped back out into the heaped-up snow in the alley behind the pub, she felt as if she might burst into tears—like some sort of adolescent.

But she held them inside.

She wasn't going to cry now.

She had *much* better options than crying.

TWO HEADS FOR
THE CHOPPING BLOCK

When **Sheilds came to,** he realised that he was hanging upside down.

He felt all the blood rushing to his skull. Swilling around his eyeballs. His heart tapped at his tonsils and a giddiness struck him with such suddenness and strength that he nearly blacked out all over again.

When he opened his eyes, he realised that he was surrounded by gloom; that the merest trickle of moonlight found its way in through the bars of his cell.

He breathed in the musky scent, and realised that it wasn't only his own odour, but that of another.

Back at Onderswort, his senses had become highly attuned. The light at Onderswort was hardly ever above a gritty twilight. Even in summer, the dirty-bottomed clouds would linger above, absorbing all the goodness from the sunlight.

Sheilds had learned to trust his sense of smell, his hearing, and what he *felt* of his surroundings just as much as he began to distrust his eyes.

He felt something binding his ankles—something sharp, and cold. *Metal.*

He imagined himself hanging from a pair of shackles above.

When he shifted his hands, hoping to reach down to the stone floor of the cell and take a little of the strain off the top of his skull, he realised that his wrists too were bound together.

Finally, he managed to twist his body in such a way that he caught sight of the other who hung up in the cell alongside him.

It took a few seconds for his brain to absorb the sight, and, when it finally did, he could hardly believe it.

Tineoots.

He hung beside him.

From his own set of shackles.

Sheilds examined Tineoots— his *brother*—for want of a better word, and he wondered just how they had caught him at last. How they had made the connection between Sheilds and Tineoots.

In retrospect Sheilds appreciated that his own theoretical escape, following the murder, had had as much to do with Tineoots keeping his nose clean as it had of keeping Sheilds out of trouble. . . out of the Gaols.

And that was where they were now, wasn't it?

Sheilds glanced back to the bars of the cell, and to the narrow, twisted stone corridor outside.

It seemed very much the same, but who was to say?

"No, not the Gaols—somewhere *else.*"

The voice took Sheilds off guard.

It sent a shudder through his chest.

And down to his gut.

When he turned, he saw that Tineoots continued to hold his eyes shut, but that he was—*apparently*—conscious.

At first Sheilds thought that he'd spoken his words aloud, and that Tineoots had overheard him.

It took Sheilds a couple of moments to realise that he had done no such thing.

Tineoots spoke again. "Mind-reading has never been a difficult task for one such as myself."

Sheilds felt his whole body go rigid.

His muscles tightened.

He stared back at Tineoots, unable to comprehend what he was saying.

This was someone just like him—someone who'd grown up *nearby* . . .

". . . Yes," Tineoots replied, "but only one of us ever had magic running through our blood; while the other—*you*—have always had something far rarer . . . a genuine lack of empathy; a strength which sees you constantly stuck between the heights of power, and . . . well, where we are right now."

Sheilds found himself stunned by Tineoots's remark. He still couldn't square what he had heard with his own ears . . . or that Tineoots had read his mind.

Although it was clearly unnecessary, Sheilds spoke out loud to Tineoots. "Where are we?" he said.

"The Palace Gaols," Tineoots replied hurriedly. "They found me out in the street, the Royal Guards; and they brought me in here, to be with you."

Despite, like Sheilds, hanging upside down from the cell, Tineoots appeared to be channelling some sort of inner-strength; a kind of inner-steel which kept his words concise and clear.

"I could have stopped them if I'd wished with my magic, but there was always the chance they would've overpowered me and killed me out on the streets of Ilsnare . . . no," he went on, "it was better that they left me with my life, and merely imprisoned me here, in the Palace Gaols."

Sheilds allowed these words to fill the cell for several seconds, and then he said, "The potion—you brewed the potion to save us from the sickness?"

Tineoots's voice gave a slight quiver. "I did more than *brew* the potion," he said, "I helped to create the sickness; the one which I hoped would account for Syre Dorf and her brother, the King, Louson." He paused. "However, it seems as though they both had some sort of exterior help—help which was beyond my control or consciousness."

"Who?" Sheilds replied.

"I believe it was Flucknor," Tineoots said, "the one who handed her a potion—her brother too. Made it so that they wouldn't suffer from the sickness."

Sheilds felt his mind weighing down his skull, almost as if—at any second—it might become so heavy as to drag him down and out of his shackles, and crumple him, head-first, onto the stone floor below.

"Didn't they . . . I mean," Sheilds said, "I thought that you were against the Creatures being given extra powers; being *accepted* into all of Ilsnare; all of Shellacnass."

Here Tineoots gave a slight chuckle.

It sounded out of place—*alien*—within the cell.

"Oh, my," Tineoots replied, "you Mortals *really are* blind to the most basic of facts; quite like the collection of Creatures; the Outcast, as they brand themselves.

"None of you ever stop to wonder—*to think*—just who might be running things in the Kingdom of Shellacnass; do you really think that mightier *Magical* beings would stand by and allow *Mortals* to keep their hold on the Kingdom? Why, at this moment, a pair of *mages*—brother and sister—are King and Princess of the entire Kingdom. Does nobody ever stop to wonder *why* the Magical wouldn't be *hiding* behind the scenes, controlling everything after all?"

Although Sheilds knew that he no longer possessed his needle, he felt as if it was strapped to his body, just beneath the material of his tunic . . . and that . . . *if only* . . . if he could *only* free his hands he might be able to slip it out.

". . . Yes," Tineoots said, "that's right . . . magic, when properly harnessed, can really be unbelievably powerful, even if it only serves to pull the wool over others' eyes."

Sheilds shifted in his bindings, feeling himself swinging lightly from one side to the other. And then he knew he needed to ask the question. "The Council of Wisemen," he said, "*Who* are they?"

Here Tineoots paused for a very long time indeed. "Well, let me put it this way," Tineoots said, "They're not all *Mortals*."

Sheilds could feel his needle up against his body all the stronger.

He just needed one hand.

Just *one* hand.

Then he would be able to reach it.

There was one more question on Sheilds's mind.

"What . . ." Sheilds said, "What *are* you?"

Tineoots said nothing by way of reply.

But Sheilds was aware of the rubbing sound of metal on metal.

All of a sudden, he could feel the shackles on his wrists coming loose.

And then his ankles.

He hardly had a second's thought before he felt himself falling—*down*—onto the stone floor of the cell. He just about had the presence of mind to put his hands out to break his tumble.

When he lay on the floor, he rested there for several moments, his mind feeling as if it was becoming unstitched—*frayed.*

And then he stared back at Tineoots, who, with a far more graceful action, swung himself down from the shackles, and landed on his feet; spread a perfect shoulder-width apart.

Finally, he looked back to Sheilds. "What am I?" he said, a smile beginning to curl his lips. "Wouldn't *you* like to know?"

Sheilds was on the point of demanding that Tineoots tell him exactly what he was when he felt a single drop of blood roll down his chest. When he reached to his tunic, to the lump which he'd been *sure* was his needle, he found that—*indeed*—it was.

He took hold of the handle, gripped it tightly in his fist; and slowly, feeling unsure on his feet, he straightened up into a standing position.

As he stood before Tineoots, waiting for him to reveal himself, Sheilds breathed in the coppery scent of his own blood.

Somehow, he got the impression that his work in Ilsnare—all his *killing*—had only just begun . . . and that there was *so much* more to come.

AN OVERHEARD CONVERSATION

When Syre found herself back in the Palace, she expected to feel exhausted. Her magic always seemed to wear her out. She had spent a long time transformed into her crow state this evening; and then there had also been the wintery weather to contend with.

Now, though, she was back in the Palace . . . back *home*, for want of a better word.

She stalked the shadowy corridors, flanked only by the odd Royal Guard, who nodded at her from their nooks and crannies, here or there, scattered about the Palace.

Her heart was thumping low and hard; and she felt as if she might lose control at any second. That the prickle of the ice magic within her veins might simply be too much for her to take any longer.

That it would—*finally*—consume her whole.

What was the point?

She had been outcast by the Outcast, and neither would she be accepted by Mortals if she allowed them to know who she truly was.

In short, she was *nowhere* . . . and *nobody.*

Was she—Syre Dorf—even *worth* saving?

As she strode along, she couldn't shift the idea of her magic consuming her utterly; that she might allow it to simply take her over.

Wouldn't it be a relief?

Like a horse which has staggered so far into the desert—parched for days—and finally tumbles down into the sand, giving itself up to the sun and dehydration.

She was at the base of the staircase to her quarters when she overheard familiar voices.

Sully.

Rut.

Her brother—*the King*—Lou.

Syre paused, thought about evading the conversation, and heading up to bed.

She didn't want to raise questions about what she was doing up and about in the Palace at this hour; if one of the more gossipy guards didn't get to Lou first.

In the end, though, she decided that she might as well tell them good night once more.

Even though Tineoots was in the Palace Gaols now, and scheduled to be executed in the morning, she had to uphold some *base* standard of being a princess.

As she passed by another few sets of Royal Guards, arriving to the kitchens, something deep within her told her to stop. That she should come to a halt.

Without a thought, she obeyed.

She pressed her back up against the stone wall.

Felt the solidity—and the *chill*—of its surface against her spine.

On the air, she could smell roast pork, and she knew that Lou had been treating their friends to something of a feast . . . and why not? They had travelled an awfully long way to arrive back at Ilsnare; and they *had* gone to the trouble of saving her life.

From the sounds of things, the three of them had got through with their eating for the evening and were now speaking together in the soft candlelight of the kitchen.

Again without a conscious thought entering her mind, Syre reached out an invisible hand and snuffed the flickering torch which hung off the wall opposite.

The flame disappeared soundlessly with a plume of white smoke.

She turned her attention back to the conversation.

Back to Lou's voice; to Sully and Rut's voices.

It was Rut who spoke first, in that round-bellied, *jolly* way of his. She could tell from his tone that he had been well fed, and—perhaps—had partaken of a flask or two of wine.

". . . What you're *saying*," Rut said, "is that you were *wrong?*"

Syre strained her hearing, which seemed amplified now that she had brought the darkness in around her, like a thick, silk blanket.

"What I'm saying," Lou said, "is that the situation has changed."

Sully was next to speak. "I don't understand *how* . . . those two, the two which we caught tonight, they'll be gone by first light tomorrow."

"It's not about them," Lou replied, "it's about the threat they *represent.*"

Syre felt as if a chilly hand took hold of her shoulder. It seemed to squeeze her almost too tightly for her to bear. The chill of her ice magic twitched about her veins. And it felt as if she might have a rush of blood to the head coming on.

She held herself still and continued to listen.

"It sounds to me," Rut went on, his voice still sounding jolly—*too jolly for the subject matter*—"as if you're trying to repress dissent . . . isn't that what you once said you *never* wanted to do?"

There was silence for a long time.

Sully picked up the thread of Rut's words. "Wasn't that the whole reason why you entrusted the security of the Webbing Armoury to us—so that you wouldn't be able to get hold of the artefacts in a time such as this?"

Syre felt as if a horse had kicked her in the stomach.

All the air leaked out of her lungs.

She thought back on what Lou had said, about him not so much as trusting himself. She realised that he had meant those words in a literal manner; that he had turned over the location of the Webbing Armoury to Rut and Sully; his two most trusted of allies.

Somehow she felt better about things . . . about him keeping the location of the Webbing Armoury from her . . . because he had also kept it from himself.

"No," Rut replied, "I don't see the reason; remember what you said, that the two of us had to remain vigilant, that we needed to keep a good eye on your behaviour, on how you *acted* whenever the Webbing Armoury was mentioned?"

Rut paused for a long moment and Syre wondered if it was because he felt his brandy wine, or ale, rising up inside his chest.

"Well, let me tell you," Rut continued, "right now, you're acting in exactly the manner which'd lead us to suspect this is for personal reasons."

Another silence drifted down over the kitchen.

Syre tasted a touch of bile at the back of her throat. She wondered if the chicken broth she'd got down at *The Soore Whip* had still been suitable for consumption.

They wouldn't have stooped so low as to try and poison her.
Would they?

Knowing that the Creatures—the *Outcast*—had been responsible for the sickness made her think that she couldn't trust *anything* they did or said.

But, in that case, who *could* she trust?

After the lengthy silence, Lou struck up the conversation again. "I can't tell you just what leads me to believe that Ilsnare is under imminent attack, but I can *feel* it . . . stronger than ever; never before was it as strong as this . . . not for a decade or more."

"Listen," Rut shot back, "even if we did believe that your need's authentic—that you truly need to get to the Webbing Armoury—it'd take days for us to reach it."

Syre allowed herself to exhale.

Her ribcage rose up and then fell down; almost as if collapsing.

Except for that remark, neither Rut or Sully had anything to say to Lou's claims, although Syre could already tell that they were doubting him, that they didn't believe one word which came out of his mouth.

And why should they?

They weren't magical like she and Lou were.

They didn't *appreciate* the importance of being in touch with the magic which dwelled in the blood; in heeding its warnings, or else paying attention to the signals.

Although Rut and Sully didn't believe Lou, Syre knew that she—*herself*—very much did. And what was more, now she better understood why Lou had kept himself to himself; why he had shuttered himself off from the world; why he had shuttered himself off from Syre. He had wanted to keep his magical instincts pure and focussed. He had wanted to keep his *ear* to the ground, so to speak.

To channel into anything which might bring the Crystal City under threat.

And if Lou said an attack on Ilsnare was imminent then who was she to argue?

Arguing would only waste time.

Now she needed to *act.*

Or else all she had grown to love—*to treat as home*—would be lost.

COUNCIL OF WISEMEN

Syre thought long and hard about what she was going to do. She hardly slept at all during the night.

At the back of her mind she couldn't shake the knowledge that she would be witnessing an execution soon after dawn. That was one of the many factors which kept her awake.

It was only when the first sunrays glimmered at the horizon that she decided it was time for her to take action. That if Rut and Sully were going to stand in the way of protecting Ilsnare—even if it was unintentional—Syre would need to do the work for herself.

Syre hoisted on Lou's sheepskin cloak and instantly felt the thick fleece up against her skin, keeping her warm, keeping the chill out. She glanced out through the windows, and down to the stables and the courtyard below. As with the other executions which she'd been forced into watching—as a Royal Witness—it would soon take place there.

But let *Lou* witness the putting-to-death of Tineoots and the assassin from the night before.

The thoughts on Syre's mind were *far* from murder.

Syre weaved her way through the Palace without intervention from anybody. She supposed that it would take time to replace Tineoots with a suitable candidate; and hopefully one who wouldn't be quite so treacherous. She had never liked Tineoots, not even from the start, and her instinct had been proven true then; just as she hoped it would be proven true now.

The streets of Ilsnare were deserted.

With the illness still very much passing through the air, she knew that all those who had some sense in them remained indoors. The ones who didn't—the ones who simply *had* to leave their homes in order to put food in their families' mouths—hadn't yet got themselves up from bed.

Syre expected to find herself crossing paths with one or two Death Carts, but she was surprised to find that not even those macabre contraptions were about during the dawn.

As she went along, watching her breath form clouds before her mouth, and feeling the early-morning chill bring a tingle out of her cheeks, she was aware of the fledgling sunlight sparking the glass rooftops into a sort of *blaze* . . . she recalled back when she'd been a little girl and she'd heard the hobblesmen blab on about Ilsnare in their tales; and she recalled how she'd never quite been able to bring herself to believe that the rooftops were *really* made of glass . . . it all seemed too much of a fantasy . . . too *unreal* to be true.

And yet it was.

When Syre finally arrived outside the Galleries of Justice, there was a scattering of people about the street. People who needed to attend the Galleries by way of obligation. She looked to their neat, formal robes; all of them sober shades of emerald, or ruby, or else *black.*

All of them the Representatives for the various criminals who would move through this organisation.

She thought about how Tineoots and the would-be assassin hadn't so much as had the chance to pass through the Galleries . . . they had been quickly dealt with on the King's Order . . . heavens knew, Syre never would've authorised an execution on her word, even if the perpetrators had attempted to have her killed.

There was just something *unnatural* about killing.

About *having* killed.

She hoped that she would never personally experience the feeling.

It wasn't difficult for Syre to get herself up to the seventh floor of the Galleries, where the Council of Wisemen sat. And it was easier still for her to get in through the door.

Before she knew it she stood in front of the seven members of the Council—three men and four women—all of them silver-haired and with infinitely *wizened* expressions seemingly engrained upon their leathery faces.

Until she stood right before them, with their round, glassy eyes upon her, she hadn't quite decided what she would say.

Officially, neither her or Lou were mages any longer; the populace had been fed the lie that Lou had never in fact been Magical, and that he had simply been a Mortal who'd come across a group of magical artefacts.

The fact that any Mortal so much as placing a *fingernail* on either the Webbing Blade, Bow or Cloak would lead to instant death was a point all but completely lost on the citizens of Ilsnare.

Not that Syre could entirely blame them.

After all, she had been like them once.

Ignorant.

The Council of Wisemen listened to her with delicate care, all of them with their faces angled in her direction. She realised that she must seem somewhat full of herself from their perspective. This young girl—*princess or not*—standing before them and claiming to have some kind of idea about governance. Her last interaction with them, of course, had been the decree she had sent across declaring that they *do not* allow Creatures or Magical beings rights.

Once Syre had got through with her explanation, and hinted at the idea that the Council should think about putting together a garrison force at the soonest possible moment, she was distracted by one of the women sat just beside her.

The woman wore robes of gold, and had on a crimson tunic underneath.

Although she had grey hair, her skin seemed quite youthful; free of wrinkles and not yet with the leathered look that many of the other members of the Council already bore.

"I think," the woman said, "that you might well be mistaken, Your Majesty."

Although Syre told herself that she needed to be diplomatic, that she needed to keep a cool head, she couldn't help it. "No," Syre said, "you've *got* to listen to me."

The woman held up a hand, and, with a smile, she shook her head. "Please, Your Majesty, if you'll listen for one moment." She paused for a second, allowing the whole room to seep into silence, as if this was some sort of method of asserting dominance. "I do believe that you're still reeling from the assassination attempt last night and, I think my fellow Council members will share my shock that such an attack was allowed to take place."

There was a murmur about the table.

The woman continued, "That being the case, I should think that it wouldn't be completely out of the ordinary that Her Majesty is currently experiencing a sort of stress which is impeding her thinking; and, which, I hasten to add, might be contributing to some form of paranoia." The woman turned back to Syre, a look of condescension smeared all over her face. "I think it would be in the best interests of Your Highness to return to the Palace and take to bed, until such a time as Her energies have been replenished."

Syre felt as if the whole of the room was staring at her; as if they all longed for her to leave so that they might laugh as the door slammed shut on her heels.

But she wouldn't give them the pleasure.

She wanted answers, and she wanted them *now.*

Thinking quickly, she said, "I want to withdraw my objection to the law which would permit Creatures the freedom to roam and be integrated throughout Ilsnare."

A stony silence ripped through the room.

Syre's gaze drifted along the elderly faces, taking them in one at a time, on some level convinced that it she could show *just one* of these members of the Council that she was truly serious then she might be able to get somewhere after all.

But none of them would hold her gaze.

It was as if her eyeballs had been transplanted an inch above her scalp.

Seeing that she wasn't managing to get the intended effect, Syre added a weak, "*Please.*"

The woman from before spoke up again. "Your Highness, I'm afraid that the time to discuss that matter has now passed, and until it is brought up by the citizens of Ilsnare that is where it shall remain." She broke into a smirk. "A Royal Decree cannot be thrown about in the breeze like loose grains of wheat."

Syre felt her chest tighten.

Her blood prickled with anger.

She couldn't believe the nerve of this woman, who was clearly deciding to bring up Syre's humble upbringing—that her brother Lou had once strived in the fields.

But that was surely far more honest work than any member of the Council had ever been involved with.

She had nothing to be ashamed of.

Syre stood firm, though.

She wouldn't turn her back on the Council.

"It's my belief that everybody, all throughout Ilsnare, through the Crystal City, should be treated equally. With the same respect. We shouldn't be damning the Magical and the Creatures to the periphery of the world."

There was a long, drawn-out silence.

Finally the woman spoke again. "Perhaps, ma'am, the Magical, and the *Creatures*, are not so far away as you may believe." She took a deep breath, looked about the Council, and then added, "As you and your brother know yourselves; magic is *very far* from skulking away in the shadows."

Syre felt her whole body become rigid.

Then she stared out across the Council.

The woman had come too far . . . too far for *her* to take.

She needed to be taught a lesson—*somehow*.

But the woman wasn't finished. "And it would be somewhat foolish to think that magic doesn't exist at every single level of Mortal authority."

"What'd you mean?" Syre found herself saying.

Missing the obvious truth for the first few heartbeats.

And then it all sunk in.

MAGICAL ADMINISTRATORS

S yre gazed about the room with new eyes, taking on board just what it was that the woman had said; in effect that all seven of the members of the Council of Wisemen, all those sat about in this room, were Magical . . . mages . . . Creatures too?

Her heart beat against her ribcage.

The ice magic prickled through her body.

She wished that she could escape the room.

Suddenly the walls seemed to be shrinking.

And all of the faces, all of the Wisemen sat in their seats around the table, seemed to be waiting on her.

Waiting . . . for *what?*

Finally, she managed to get a hold on herself—and her *tongue.* "You had the chance to approve the law, and you didn't," Syre said. "I got in the way, made it so that it wouldn't happen. You must all be . . . *furious*," she settled with.

Nobody replied to this comment.

Syre waited for one of them to speak up, perhaps for one of them to hurl a hex in her direction as if confirming the very worst of her suspicions.

But they remained silent.

"Please," she said, feeling a fresh wave of desperation slowly rising up from her gut; almost like a sickness, like the sickness she had suffered from before being administered with the potion. "*Forgive me*," she finished.

Again, nobody among the Council spoke, until the woman from before stepped in.

She slipped Syre a smile and said, "Come now, you must understand that everything happens for a reason. From your time in the Palace you must have an inkling that such powers wouldn't be granted you and your brother without it being easily checked . . . easily *countered*."

"I don't follow," Syre replied, honestly.

"No," the woman said, with a thin-lipped smile, "I don't suppose you do."

Syre, again, took exception to the woman's tone.

More than anything, she wanted to reach out and throttle her.

Or, perhaps, leave her scrabbling about on her back—helpless as a cockroach; and as easily picked up off the floor by a swift and deadly crow swooping down.

The woman continued, "Think to yourself, who *authored* that Royal Decree? Who was the one who *had* you sign the Decree?"

Syre replied without thinking, "Tineoots."

And as Syre thought it over, as she thought through the pieces of the puzzle, a realisation dawned over her. Tineoots had been in control the whole time, and he had been working in cahoots with the Council of Wisemen.

But *why?*

She shook her head, unable to understand it.

"How come you all, being Magical, wanted to make it so that others might not be free to roam Ilsnare?"

The woman held Syre's gaze. "Because," she replied, "the only advantage the Magical *ever* have in this world is when they're subtle—when they're kept underground." She held out her hand, the palm outstretched. "If, for example, the Mortals were to find out that the Council of Ilsnare is in fact staffed with Magical beings then what do you think would happen?"

"There'd be a revolution," Syre replied, her voice dampened down.

"And," the woman continued, "more to the point, if we were to make it so that Magical beings—and *Creatures*—were allowed to freely roam the streets of Ilsnare it would normalise magic, and soon reveal to the general populace the *truth* about their Council."

Syre felt as if her mind was coming apart.

But she held herself still.

Determined not to become overwhelmed.

"No," the woman said, "it was of vast importance that we keep the secret concealed, despite the wishes of the people in bringing this matter to the attention of the Council." She paused for a long moment. "Do you see that now?"

Syre stared down at the slicked-up surface of the table before her. No longer was there a cutting, sarcastic edge to the woman's tone . . . her voice had become more matter of fact now.

Syre found herself replying, "Yes, I understand."

As Syre stood there, thinking through her next move, something struck her.

And she glanced up at the Council.

"What about Flucknor? Tineoots threatened me with him . . . with something *happening* to him if I didn't do what he said. What will happen to him now?"

"Nothing," the woman replied, with a smirk, "as long as he keeps his mouth shut—as long as *both* of you keep your mouths shut. As long as that organisation which he is involved with continues to be weak, and ineffectual."

Although Syre soon realised that she should've said nothing at all, she couldn't help blurting out the words before thinking. "They were the ones responsible for the sickness—the one which still sweeps through Ilsnare."

Again, the woman smirked in response. "No," she said, "Tineoots was the one who was responsible *for that.*"

Syre allowed this particular fact to resound about the inside of her skull. "If you're working with Tineoots, if you have been all this time, then why're you having him put to death?"

The woman shook her head. "We're not—he will have escaped by now."

Right then, it was as if a large, invisible hole opened up around Syre.

And she realised that she was surrounded by enemies.

On all sides.

RAMPAGE IN THE PALACE

S heilds couldn't quite conceal his glee as he strode alongside Tineoots, through the cobbled courtyard of Il-snare Palace.

He'd believed that he would never breathe the air of freedom again ever since he arrived to Onderswort. And it'd seemed that he had breathed his last when he'd been sent to the Gaols for killing that man-boy.

Then once more, for a third—and *final* time—when he'd been locked up with Tineoots in the Palace Gaols.

But he was out now.

He had escaped.

Tineoots had broken them out.

Sheilds stretched his mind back to precisely how it had happened; how the two of them had been shackled, and then how their shackles had seemed almost to fall away as Tineoots had performed his magic.

Sheilds recalled, as they had been fleeing the cell, headed along the corridor and toward freedom, how he had slipped a sidelong glance to Tineoots.

For once, he had observed Tineoots in his true form, the form which he really was—beneath the human flesh which he summoned so convincingly.

Sheilds supposed that the magic Tineoots had used to spring them free of the gaol had taken its toll on his ability to maintain his illusion of being Mortal.

He had looked to Tineoots and, first, seen the red, *raw* skin.

And then his enormous claws; and the spines which grew out of his back and which slunk about, one into the other.

Tineoots's appearance had reminded him of a lizard's head placed on a bear's body . . . only a bear stripped of all its fur; and left only with mottled scabs and hardened flesh beneath.

Those fangs had been sharp, and had a cutting-edge to rival the nib of Sheilds's needle . . . the needle which Tineoots had somehow conjured onto his body.

Now, though, at this moment in time, Tineoots had returned to his human form, and was striding alongside Sheilds; expressionless and determined.

When Sheilds had asked Tineoots what their plan would be next, Tineoots had said that he was going to kill the King; and that he was going to take his 'rightful' place.

He had admitted that it had taken a decade of planning since Lou had taken over Ilsnare Palace, and it'd taken him a long while to decide on making his move.

Tineoots had been concerned about something he termed the 'Webbing Armoury' . . . magical artefacts which apparently had the power to defeat an army of mages; let alone a Creature such as Tineoots—more accustomed to harnessing raw magic; using his magic on impulse; than with any degree of carefully calculated control.

But now the time had come.

When he could be assured that Lou was no longer a threat.

That he was little more than a Mortal soul to be *taken . . .*

As these thoughts passed through Sheilds's mind, he wondered what his role might be in Tineoots's new administration. Perhaps he would return to the Eye in some sort of a senior role . . . it was strange, although Sheilds almost never thought of anything with regards to more than a few hours hence, he couldn't help but lose himself in fantasies surrounding what might await him in the near-future.

Because, now, for the first time in his life, it seemed as though he *had* a future.

Sheilds was dimly aware of a kerfuffle from above. He twisted his neck upward to take a look and saw, on the ramparts, a pair of Royal Guards pointing crossbows in their direction.

As Sheilds stared at the tip of the bolt, resting on the taut cable, ready to fling forward out of the mechanism, he felt every muscle in his body stiffen.

He listened to the distinct *click* of the trigger.

And he waited for the burning-hot sensation of the sharpened metal point entering his skin . . . perhaps his neck.

His *throat.*

But nothing happened.

As Sheilds stood still, he realised that he had closed his eyes; so convinced had he become of his fate. He had thought that this—*really*—would be the end.

Not quite yet, though, it seemed.

When he finally reopened his eyes, he saw that a translucent sphere had formed around them. It appeared to have the consistency and sheen of a bubble off a bucket of soap suds. He realised now that the Royal Guards hadn't just fired one crossbow bolt at them—*the escapees*—but *several.*

And that they were still firing.

Sheilds watched on from behind the film of the protective bubble which Tineoots had cast, and he saw the crossbow bolts tinkling down onto the cobblestones outside; all of them about as harmful as a swarm of flies.

He turned to look at Tineoots, expecting to see him wrestling with this protective charm—because that was surely what it was.

But, instead, Tineoots had a wide smile curling back his lips.

It stretched all the way up to his eyes.

And as Tineoots held the two of them safe within the bubble, Sheilds noticed how the Mortal projection he cast over himself flickered several times; revealing the mottled flesh and hardened scabs on his face beneath.

Never before had Tineoots realised that magic dwelled so close.

That, even as a child, on Guider Street, it had been so near that he could've easily reached out to touch it . . .

BETRAYAL

Syre sprinted through the crooked, near-deserted, snow-covered streets of Ilsnare, in the direction of the Palace. The revelations following her meeting with the Council still very much clung to her conscious.

Magic.

It had been all around her; and the *whole* time . . . not just since she and Lou had arrived, but for the entire length of history, it seemed.

As Syre willed her muscles onward, already feeling a single bead of sweat trickling down her spine, despite the winter chill, and the snow all around, she thought about when she'd been a little girl; when her world had consisted of simply Endmere and—*perhaps*—the wise woman who had been the source of all her knowledge . . . and the books which she'd given her.

It was testament to Syre's day-to-day existence now that she couldn't even recall the name of the wise woman. It was almost as if Syre's past had vanished ever since she'd made a conscious decision—*months after Endmere burned down*—to simply push it to the back of her brain.

There had been other things to occupy her mind with; understanding her magic for one.

She pressed on harder still, inadvertently catching a merchant woman—one of the few souls scattered about the streets of the Crystal City—and sending her tumbling into the market stall of freshly picked apples.

As Syre turned the corner, she heard that thick—almost gut-clenchingly repulsive—*crunch* as a rogue apple was crushed beneath her boots.

And into the hard-packed snow.

It reminded her of the time she had seen a drunk man—back when they'd dwelled in the Encampments, in the foothills of the Sable Mountains—having his head crushed by a spooked horse.

Someone had said that it had been like a watermelon; but Syre had been too terrified at the time to make any sense of this comparison.

Now that she did have a little distance from that memory, and now that the apple had fallen beneath the sole of her boots, she realised it had sounded more like an apple.

Just like an apple.

Nobody had realised what she'd seen—Lou had been away with Auch'ray, his mentor, at the time. Hearing a commotion outside her tent, Syre had simply been curious. She had gone to see what all the fuss was about. And she'd taken in the drunk man stumbling about, singing to himself; providing much-needed entertainment for the other dwellers of the Encampments as he stumbled from side to side . . . but then had come the tragedy; and the laughter had stopped.

And Syre had been left with the image sketched on her mind.

Never to be removed.

As Syre neared the Palace now, she realised that she faced a far different horror; that she would need to find Tineoots, that she would have to raise the alarm, inform Lou of the threat he wielded.

She wondered if Lou would believe her at all.

Lou knew that Syre had never much liked him, but he surely believed that the crisis had been long-ago averted.

That if Tineoots had previously been a threat, then he wasn't any longer.

Syre increased her pace, and looked to the Palace Gates.

As she neared them, she noted how the streets surrounding the Palace were strangely deserted.

Usually there was the stink of all sorts of spices in the air; all sorts of fish, and meat.

There was the *babble* of conversation; the warmth from flaming stoves.

And the sight of animated merchants of wildly different complexions. Voices with diametrically opposed accents. Jabbering away in an animated fashion.

Even during the sickness, the merchants had still come.

Their livelihoods depended on their trade; so catching the illness was a risk most were willing to take.

But, today, there was nobody present at all.

It seemed so lonely; almost sad.

One of the fixed features of her time in Ilsnare, of being considered an *impromptu* member of the Royal Family, had been the consistent presence of the merchants in the street outside the Palace.

It'd made her feel somehow less exclusive, almost more *human* in some ways . . . although she realised that she was a long way from being *that*.

Syre was more surprised still to note that there were no Royal Guards on the gates to the Palace. She felt herself seething silently, and wondered if this might have been one of Tineoots's conceits; somehow from inside his gaol cell, with death lurking just around the corner, he had managed to find some sort of influence with the outside world.

Every day, she felt as if she hated that man a little more.

He had betrayed her.

He had betrayed *everyone* . . . no matter what the Council believed.

Syre passed through the corridors of the Palace, half expecting to come across citizens, with silver or gold gathered in their arms, taking the opportunity of the lack of guards on the gates to loot whatever caught their fancy.

But there was no one.

The Palace corridors were eerily quiet.

Syre prepared herself for anything which might be lurking around the stone corridors; anything at all which might leap out of the shadows.

One of the things which she hated most about Ilsnare Palace was how, even on roaring-hot summer days, the interior of the building would remain dark and cold . . . no matter how many torches were lit and kept ablaze throughout the hallways.

Why hadn't any of her predecessors thought to punch a few windows into the stonework?

Again, not finding any resistance, Syre managed to get herself up to her quarters.

Back in her bedroom, she realised that she could hear shouting.

Coming from beyond the balcony windows.

She trod over to the windows, feeling herself shaking all over— not from fear, but from barely controlled *ice magic.* She could feel it freezing up her veins now; very much in control of her heart . . . and working on her mind.

It wouldn't take too much effort . . . actually, it wouldn't take any at all . . . just for her to allow herself to let go . . . to allow her magic to *possess* her body . . . but she had to hold on . . . just for a little longer . . .

She squeezed her fingers into fists and held them down at her sides.

Outside, in the courtyard, she looked down on the unmistakable sight of a giant, powerfully cast protective bubble. A charm. And, within the bubble, she saw—*sure enough*—Tineoots; and the bald, would-be assassin.

She turned her attention up to the ramparts.

To the Royal Guards as they fired off their crossbows at the protective bubble.

And seemed to make no inroads.

What use was physical force against magic?

. . . And, thanks to the Council, Syre at least knew that the foe she was dealing with—*Tineoots*—was a Magical one.

She looked about the courtyard, as if she expected to see Lou outfitted in the Webbing Cloak; with the Webbing Bow strapped over his back and the Webbing Blade grasped down at his thigh.

But then she recalled the conversation she'd overheard between Lou, Sully and Rut.

Sully and Rut were the only ones who knew the location of the Webbing Armoury, and they hadn't been convinced Lou's need was genuine. But, even if they had been, there would've been no time for them to go and fetch the weapons.

As Syre stared on down at the courtyard, she was aware of a glimmering—almost impossibly *bright*—light at the very centre of the protective charm.

The reaction was so sudden, such a *knee-jerk* instinct, that she hardly had time to speak the words into her own mind; the ones which implored her to . . . *DUCK!!*

DEVASTATION

Sheilds felt the warmth crawling out of every pore.

It seemed as if he was immortal as he stood within the protective bubble which Tineoots had cast.

He could smell blood on the air.

Thick and bitter.

Clinging to the back of his throat.

As he stood within the protective bubble, he watched the waves of light—*all different shades of glittering gold and silver*—flood out and swarm the Royal Guards standing up on the ramparts.

Sheilds watched on as, one by one, the guards toppled over, their weapons flying out of their grasp, and landing on the stone beside their prostrate bodies.

Acting on impulse, feeling as if somebody was watching him, he turned to look up at the balcony, to Princess Syre Dorf's quarters.

To the location where he had been supposed to kill her . . . now he would get done with that task . . . *now* he would be successful.

He saw that the glass of the balcony doors had shattered, and that the fragments continued to rain down on the courtyard. Glistening in the sunlight.

There was no need for Sheilds to vocalise this desire, of course, Tineoots could simply read his thoughts.

Tineoots opened a hole in the protective charm just large enough for Shields to duck through.

When Tineoots emerged on the other side of the protective charm, he half expected a crossbow bolt to find his chest. He thought that he might feel the metal pierce his skin, take him down, lie him in the snow and have him bleed to death.

He would have had no objection.

He *could have* no objection.

He had done his work throughout his life—the work he'd felt compelled to do . . . satisfied every one of his bloodthirsty urges.

But no bolt arrived.

He continued on his way, toward the doorway of the Palace.

When he got to the corridor, out of the daylight and the range of the Royal Guards, he expected some sort of resistance.

But there was none to be found.

He merely skulked along, sticking to the stone walls, ducking out of the way of the torches hanging down, sending their flaming light about the gloom.

Back at Onderswort, he had been unable to imagine how the King of Shellacnass might live; simply *incapable* of processing that there was anything aside from the dirgy fog which swilled all about the prison colony; the endless marshland which surrounded it.

And the soggy clouds which perpetually hung above.

Just thinking about Onderswort now, he believed he could taste that slightly bitter—slightly *fishy*—flavour at the back of his throat. And he could feel the prickle of the sweat seeping out of his skin following a hard day's toil hoeing stodgy land. Some days he would feel a wound on his leg or arm which had gone untended through the day, and, lying in his bunk as the night closed in, he would suck at his affliction.

Taste his own blood.

And feel his unquenched thirst become almost unbearable.

It had been one of those particular moments when he had decided he could take no more—when he had decided that he simply had to break free of Onderswort.

He reasoned that it would be better to die in the act of escape than live out the half-life forced upon him by the prison colony.

In retrospect, and especially now, climbing the stone staircase, headed for Princess Syre Dorf's quarters, he saw that it had been the correct decision.

This was his pinnacle.

His *peak.*

The crowning glory in his murderous life.

Sheilds reached the top step of the staircase, and he glanced about, expecting to find a Royal Guard with a crossbow pointed at him. Sheilds thought that he might have a second or so to think about his life—*and how he had spent it*—one final moment to reflect on things before the guard pulled the trigger.

But, again, the corridor was deserted.

He was alone.

Free—*free*—to do as he wished.

Sheilds eyed the archway leading to Princess Syre's quarters, the pair of doors wide open. He slowed his gait, putting himself in mind of a tomcat on the prowl, stalking its prey; keeping to the shadows until it was the right moment to strike.

He felt for his needle.

He would make the death slow and painful.

Just as he liked it.

This was to be his masterwork, after all.

Earlier, when they had broken free of the Palace Gaols, he and Tineoots had agreed that Sheilds would have Syre to himself; to do whatever he wished, on the condition that Tineoots himself would be the one to face off with Lou.

Although Sheilds had agreed to this proposition, he knew that it would be a difficult matter indeed to control himself if the opportunity presented itself.

Perhaps his future, as Tineoots saw it, might never come to pass. . . . If it was so, then it was so . . .

Walking in through the doorway, Sheilds found himself struck down with a sense of . . . *something.*

Was it fear?

Last time Sheilds had entered Princess Syre's quarters it had been a trap—that pair of men had awaited him. They had *ambushed* him . . . hit him over the head.

But despite this memory, it wasn't fear . . . no, it was more akin to a feeling of *déjà vu.*

He *had* been here before, of course.

Was that it?

Was that the cause of the swilling, slightly nauseous sensation in the pit of his stomach?

He gripped the needle tighter still and fixed his thoughts on how it would feel to finally pierce the woman's lung . . . to keep her from screaming out for help.

He would enjoy watching her bleed away in silence.

On instinct, Sheilds glanced to the balcony, where he had previously seen Princess Syre standing, when he'd been down in the courtyard.

She was no longer there.

What had he expected?

That she might stand with her back to him . . . *waiting* for the torture which would eventually end her life?

Sometimes Sheilds believed himself an egotist, as if the whole world revolved around him. But he knew that he had to be more realistic in his thinking . . . this wasn't some fantasy concocted for his own amusement . . . this was the *real* world . . .

Sheilds turned his attention to the rest of the room, to the four-poster bed, and then to the dressing table. He supposed that she had been comfortable here, during her decade or so of inhabiting the Palace . . . but that stay was coming to an end now.

Forever.

Sheilds had already cast his gaze about the room a handful of times before he finally spotted Syre. He had no idea why it had taken him so long to seek her. But he *did* find her.

Over in the corner of her quarters.

Her back to him.

Staring at the wall.

Strangely, Sheilds felt his heart bob up in his throat.

His pulse pounded a little harder.

Somehow—for *some* reason—he felt a twinge of anticipation.

A sensation he'd never felt before.

He wondered if the image before him, the well-tanned shoulders presented him, the dainty black dress she wore, stoked some sort of memory he had long ago repressed.

Or had *believed* repressed.

He took a step toward her, feeling his heart tick harder still.

He gripped his needle tighter.

A bead of sweat rolled down the side of his face.

His heart sunk down to his stomach.

It gave him a ticklish sensation in his chest.

But he continued to tread forward.

This was his time—his time *now.*

He closed in on her.

Near enough to reach out and touch her skin . . . if he so wished.

He brought his needle up in his hold.

He held it at the precise angle for slipping it upward.

Into her lung.

She would hardly realise.

Not until the point of the needle came into contact with her flesh.

Sheilds wasn't sure why he paused—why he halted—but something—a sound nearby?—forced him to turn and look. It was the only time he could recall having his mind's attention distracted at the very moment of a murder.

When he turned back to Syre, she stood right before him.

Turned around.

Her eyes—*her entire eyeballs*—were black.

And her . . . her *hair* . . . it seemed almost to have taken on the texture of *feathers* . . . before Sheilds could speak, let alone act, he felt himself being pushed back, away from her, an invisible—*chilling*—hand shoving him in the centre of his chest.

He felt himself drifting backward.

His feet no longer touched the stone floor below.

Floating . . . *floating* . . . that was right.

His eyes never left *hers.*

His eyes *couldn't* leave hers.

Those pit-black eyes fastening onto his.

No end in sight.

No *soul* at the end of the tunnel.

Sheilds felt the needle slip through his fingers and—from some seemingly impossible distance away—heard it clatter at his feet.

His skull filled with a scream.

So strong that it brought his hair standing on end.

And his heart pattering harder still in his throat.

Everything played out in a kind of slow motion.

Sheilds watched on, his feet still floating above the ground, as Princess Syre rose up from her position, her black dress moving sleekly from some draught which entered the room.

He felt his head tilting backward, those same invisible chilling hands gripping him, keeping him from moving so much as a single muscle of his own volition.

It was when her body rose to the ceiling, and she needed to arch her head down toward him—those black eyes of hers gaping wide and *evil*—that he felt the screaming in his mind reach its zenith.

And he could no longer take it.

Something—*somewhere*—deep within him gave way.

And he knew it was no good.

That this was the end.

The end of his life.

Sheilds shut his eyes tight—*almost like a frightened babe*—as he heard a cacophony resembling thunder take over the inside of his mind.

And he never knew peace again.

ONE STEP FURTHER

S yre felt as if her whole body was—*all at once*—on fire and frozen solid.

She had reached out with her mind.

She had known he was coming, of course.

And, dimly now, because it was somewhere near the back of her mind, she recalled having made a conscious decision to allow her ice magic in.

To allow her ice magic to rule her veins.

It had been so simple.

Almost like clicking her fingers; or clapping her hands.

She felt stronger than ever.

As if a fountain of eternal energy flowed out from her chest, swilling about her in an invisible vent of freezing-cold air.

Buffeting her.

Keeping her from harm.

She stared out at her quarters, rendered before her now in shades of grey—*black and white.*

She looked to the would-be assassin's body.

It wasn't a pretty sight.

Blood.

Everywhere.

The body crumpled.

Useless.

That sharp 'needle' device lying beside him.

For several seconds, she wondered if she should feel pleasure—*a sense of accomplishment*—in what she had done here; in ridding the world of such a distasteful individual . . . one who would hurt any being in the world with his murderous tendencies.

And to do so, by necessity, she had had to bloody her own hands.

What did she think of that?

Muffled, near the back of her consciousness, she could feel a little voice—a *tiny* voice; almost like a canary trapped in a rickety cage—protesting in a sharp, but ultimately feeble tone.

How could that voice *ever* hope to be heard against such power?

Against the great power which flooded Syre's body?

And which now occupied her soul?

Slowly, with a gentle *hum*, like a nearby swarm of bees, the world returned to Syre's perception.

She drank in her surroundings; her brain reminding her what was taking place just beyond her balcony. In the courtyard outside.

Tineoots.

Another who needed to be taken care of.

Another *insignificant* matter.

Syre turned her attention away from the crumpled mess which had once been the man who'd tried to kill her—not once, but *twice*—and she allowed herself to float through the air, over to the balcony.

She peered out through the glass.

To the white world outside.

To the snow which was layered upon everything.

And then to the figure in the centre of the courtyard; to the doughy form of Tineoots.

He looked so *Mortal* . . . he looked as if he might be so easily beaten by one such as herself.

But something else nagged at her to take care.

Something which—*itself*—didn't wish to be destroyed.

Now, Syre could tell, she had something else inside her entirely.

Something which she couldn't define.

Ice magic?

Or something else . . .

It was almost as if a darkness lurked over her.

She imagined it in the form of a cloud.

Ready to rain down . . . to snow . . . or to *hail*.

Almost as if it was preordained, Syre watched on as Tineoots stood in the middle of the courtyard, and then, slowly—moving *so* slowly—he turned his head in her direction.

Their eyes met.

And Syre felt a fresh chill enter her heart.

As she stared at him she watched his flesh lose its solid form.

It became transparent.

First she noted, growing out from his hands, spiny, sharpened claws.

Next there were the spines which grew up and out of his back.

Finally there was the head.

It reminded Syre of a lizard.

Those beady, swivelling eyes.

Fixed on her.

She knew that he was a beast.

A *Creature*.

One which she had seen before.

Just like Brotsboore.

He was *just like* Brotsboore.

Now she had allowed the control of her magic to slip it would take all the strength within her to channel her power in Tineoots's direction.

To strike him down.

For good.

SHOWDOWN

Syre knew that she couldn't hide.

But, what was more, she had no intention of hiding.

Why should she with the kind of power which dwelled within her?

The confidence which now flowed through her blood.

Why, she was convinced that—*if she so willed it*—she could strike any being she wished from the face of the Earth.

. . . If they only stood up before her.

Tineoots stood before her now.

Syre willed the balcony doors open.

They flew off their hinges.

Blasted out into the frozen air ahead of her.

She was half aware of them tumbling down.

Of them *crunching* as they landed on the whited-out world below.

Then she stood out on the balcony.

Her sights fixed on Tineoots.

That protective charm which swelled about him.

A translucent sphere.

Its sheen in the bright daylight.

Taking on the reflection of the snow.

First things first.

She held herself still in the air, floating up off the floor. Allowed herself to stabilise.

To become *normalised* to the sensation.

It was important that she be comfortable in her own skin.

That would be her edge seeing as Tineoots was still hiding in another's skin.

A *Mortal's* skin.

As Syre descended through the air, approaching the courtyard down below, she thought of how much energy it had sapped from her when she'd transformed into a crow . . . and then she wondered where Tineoots had scavenged the required energy to transform himself into a Mortal.

Away from his brutish, *true* form.

It made her head spin.

And it allowed doubts to creep into her mind.

But she tried to block them out as well as she could.

Now was hardly the time for doubts.

The soles of Syre's boots landed in the fresh layer of snow which lined the courtyard. She listened to the distant-sounding *crunch* as they met with the iced-over surface. Although she didn't so much as look around, she knew that the Royal Guards had been flattened by the hexes which Tineoots had cast.

She was alone here.

Just her and Tineoots.

Somewhere—*somehow*—she knew that it would come to this.

And it had.

She closed the gap on Tineoots, watching him protected by the charm which he'd conjured. She knew just what to do to break such a charm, although she hoped that he might do the honour-able thing; that he might meet her in a duel instead of hiding away.

At least that was how she'd read about it in books.

In the Palace Library she'd scoured volumes on magical history, gone investigating all the norms and ritual involved in a magical duel. But those tomes had only dealt with mage-on-mage duels; never, so far as she could tell, with a mage fighting a Creature.

Perhaps someone would write a tome on that subject when this fight was over.

Syre breathed in deeply, right to the very pits of her lungs; in the way which she had learned was the most effective means to chan-nel her magical strength.

And then, when she felt like she might be about to burst, she breathed out.

CLOUD OF ICE AND DARKNESS

Syre held her eyes locked tight for the first several moments as she breathed out.

It helped her concentration.

When she did open her eyes, she noted the extra bite in the air, the way that it nibbled at her cheeks, and how she now felt her blood prickling at the insides of her veins as if desperate to escape. She stared out at the steam which'd emerged from her pert lips, and watched as the grey cloud—crackling with what appeared almost like a thunderstorm—swilled in the direction of Tineoots, and his protective charm.

The cloud bundled over and around itself, constantly on the move.

Never the same shape for longer than a second.

She had learned this hex in one of the many magical books in the Palace Library; in the section which'd been cordoned off and marked as being 'RESTRICTED'.

But there had been no *other* attempts at security.

In the dead of night, those times when she felt the ice magic at its strongest, stirring in her body, refusing to allow her to sleep, she would sneak out of her quarters and wander through the night-time Palace to the Library . . . and she would learn something more.

Why she'd chosen this particular hex as the means of breaking through Tineoots's defences, she couldn't quite say. Only that it'd *seemed* the correct spell to cast.

She watched on as the cloud bundled about Tineoots, swirling over the protective charm, corroding that sleek, bubble-like glean of the surface; first making it dull, and then clearly creating pock-marks—*holes*—in the façade.

When the first tendrils of the cloud breached the protective charm, she observed the expression on Tineoots's face—his *real* face—and she observed the protective charm fail.

She stood back as Tineoots fell to his knees.

Apparently exhausted.

Syre could feel her heart beating hard in her throat.

Her blood swelled in her temples.

And her whole body grew rigid.

Her muscles *freezing* tight.

This couldn't be it . . . it couldn't have been *this* easy . . . could it?

Syre held back for another few moments, expecting Tineoots to rise up, to return to his feet at any second. But he remained crouched down, his energy apparently spent.

Syre, though, wouldn't be so easily fooled.

When she did tread forward, it was with a great sense of apprehension.

Her heartbeat slowed.

She willed it that way—*almost consciously.*

As she got closer to Tineoots, she could hear his heavy breathing.

And that his façade—the *physical* façade he had put on for who knew how many years—had faded completely. Now he inhabited his true form.

A large-chested Creature with the head of a lizard.

And with scaled—or *scabbed?*—skin.

What took Syre most off guard was Tineoots's emaciated frame.

Whenever she'd pictured Tineoots in her mind before, she'd always thought of him having that merry, jiggling gut of his. Those pudgy cheeks which went to show that he spent a great deal of his downtime in the Palace Kitchens, stuffing his face.

But that had all been an act.

For the sick creature within.

As she grew closer to Tineoots, she noted the sulphuric stench clinging to the air.

Almost like rotten eggs.

It reminded her of something . . . or was it *someone?*

She couldn't quite square the recollection with the sensory detail.

Not right away, in any case.

Soon, Syre stood over Tineoots. She bore down on him, feeling almost like those cruel children she'd witnessed throughout Ilsnare who might crowd around an ants' nest, their feet held above the ants, ready to bring their full force down on the insects.

To bring about their doom.

The level of cruelty displayed in those children made her shudder. Even now.

Just to think about it.

As she stood over him, Tineoots's voice croaked free from his throat.

He stared up at her with his black—*black*—eyes.

And she felt the weakness in Tineoots . . . how she might be able to reach out, wrap her hands about his lizard throat and squeeze the last of the life out of him.

It would be simple.

So simple.

So why couldn't she bring herself to administer the killing stroke?

UNSEEN ALLIES

S yre held off and she listened to Tineoots speak.

He spoke directly to her.

Into her *mind . . .*

— Never before have I felt such . . . such strength. Such Magical strength.

Although Syre had learned about mind-reading, she hadn't often practised it.

She had always been afraid, even in the small hours of the morning, creeping about the streets of Ilsnare, that her brother would somehow find the truth . . . find out that she had been practising a *dark* magic skill.

But she had studied enough of the theory to know how to transmit her thoughts steadily and clearly. She spoke back to him:

— Dark magic is a vast and largely untapped well.

There was a pause and Syre could feel the pain flooding through Tineoots's body. She felt it coming—*wave-upon-wave*—never ceasing.

He wasn't far from death now.

When she looked over him, looked over his skin, she saw how the icicles of her dark magic cloud gathered about his skin; slowly stopping all of the vital functions of his body.

Even if she'd wanted to, she wouldn't be able to halt the process now.

It was well beyond her own abilities of healing charms.

She had dedicated much more of the late-night studies to other—*less subtle*—skillsets.

And ones which, broadly speaking, brought about pain.

But she wouldn't allow him to die before she'd got more information.

She spoke to him within her own mind once again:

— *The Council of Wisemen. They have the Magical among them. Is that as far as the corruption goes?*

Even despite his condition, the fact that Tineoots lay there, in his red-raw, lizard-like body, dying before her, Syre interpreted something like a smirk in her own mind, communicated to her from Tineoots.

Then he answered her.

— *Here and there; here and there. Magic has always dwelled; and forever will continue to do so. In Ilsnare, and out . . . all throughout Shellacnass. It doesn't take some* law *to allow magic into the midst of Mortals; it shall always be. The trick, though, well, that lies in misinformation, in never allowing the Mortals to know* exactly *just where the magic dwells.*

Syre thought about this, she thought back to what the Council of Wisemen had told her; about how they'd treated her like some naïve little girl . . . and, well, was she anything except for that?

She had believed herself alone, to be one of the handful of magic practitioners throughout the Crystal City.

Now, though, of course, she knew much better.

It was much more than a mere *handful.*

Syre turned her attention back to Tineoots:

— *I'll tell them. I'll tell them what's going on. That there's magic surrounding us.*

Tineoots remained down at her feet, his body still rising and falling with quickening breathing as death crept ever closer. He replied to her, in her mind once again:

— *Let me tell you about my people; Syre . . .*

She noted that he no longer referred to her as either "Your Majesty" or as "ma'am" . . . he had given up on those pretences. The truth was out in the open now. And they might as well speak frankly . . . without the adornments.

Tineoots continued:

— *Thousands and thousands of years ago we emerged from the Sable Mountains; a small tribe, no larger than thirty or forty of us. Where we originally came from; where our homeland resides; we have no idea. There are theories, of course, but no facts. No written history. My people have no written language. We have never needed it.*

Syre felt her chest tighten.

She could still feel the magic prickling through her body.

She could feel its ebb and flow; how it seemed to suck at her insides, as if feeding off her physical strength. She wished that she might be able to check her magic somehow; that there might be some means for her to curtail its advancement.

Something so simple as tugging on a horse's reins and bringing it to a halt.

Tineoots went on:

— *Shape-shifters; that's what we are. The one ability which allowed us to travel throughout Mortal communities; which allowed us to meld into their societies seamlessly. We travelled on their coattails. Together with Mortals we helped to construct settlements. We aided with the construction of Ilsnare; with the Crystal City. However you would wish to see it, however Mortals would wish to see it, my kind are as tangled up within Mortal history as horses.*

An unseen ally.

Syre couldn't allow herself to stay quiet now, even though she could feel the ice magic swilling through her almost like an un-stoppable nausea.

She spoke back to him:

— *If you truly are their allies then why do you continue to deceive them; Mortals; why do you dwell within their communities without allowing your presence to be known?*

Tineoots replied:

— *Because they are too foolish to know any different; to under-stand our importance to them. We are all that keeps the* Magical *from crushing them, from crushing all that they have built.*

Feeling that speaking within her own mind was now as natural as speaking with her tongue, Syre shot back:

— *How do you know that?*

Tineoots remained quiet for several moments and Syre almost convinced herself that he had faded away; that he had slipped away into death.

Finally, he replied:

— *I kept an eye on you and your brother, didn't I? I kept the two of you in check, kept the two of you from damaging the Crystal City, from bringing the whole place to its knees.*

Although Syre wanted to fight back, wanted to tell him that this was a lie, she couldn't help but think of her quarters; only minutes ago now; when she had mercilessly killed that would-be assassin.

That she had felt the anger—and the *fear*—rip through her heart.

The overwhelming darkness.

When her power had got out of control, she had *killed* a Mortal . . . did it really matter whether or not she might've been right or wrong?

Tineoots continued:

— *I was biding my time. I wanted to wait until I was sure that your brother hadn't access to the Webbing Armoury . . . that would be my time to strike; my time to knock the two of you from the Throne; and to appoint somebody worthier.*

Syre replied without thinking; speaking aloud, "Who?"

— *A Mortal.*

The way that Tineoots's words formed in Syre's mind were so matter of fact, and delivered so calmly, that she could hardly bring herself to believe that he was on anything *but* the side of good.

And—*surely*—the Kingdom of Shellacnass would be better served with a Mortal on the throne . . . she, being the reluctant princess, was surely the greatest proof of that.

Syre could feel the beating of Tineoots's heart growing weaker by the second; and she knew that he would soon slip away from her; that he would soon slip away from this world; from this reality.

But she couldn't allow him to leave her without asking the question:

— *Your breed, your* race, *what is your name?*

She felt an almost self-satisfied drawing-in of breath from Tineoots, and then she heard him reply into her mind:

— *The Horrox.*

And, even though Syre knew that it was only a name, she felt a shudder pass through her body.

All the way down, to the base of her spine

Where it chilled her like ice.

WALKING IN WEAKNESS

As far as possible, Syre kept her mind occupied for the following few weeks.

She made a point of keeping out of her brother—Lou's—way.

Nobody had witnessed her showdown with Tineoots. All of the Royal Guards who had stood up on the ramparts had been rendered unconscious.

They retained no memory of the incident.

All they knew, as they had returned to their feet—blinking rapidly, their hearts going *pitter-pat*—was that Syre stood over Tineoots's dead body.

And since Syre had been the only one to hear Tineoots's words within her mind, she found that she constantly shook herself—*mentally*—trying to work out whether or not what she had heard in her own mind had actually happened at all.

Perhaps she had put those words into Tineoots's mind, metaphorically speaking.

Or perhaps not...

While Syre was up in her quarters one day, with the gloomy, grisly-grey clouds bearing down on the courtyard, and the snow piled up to the edges of the walls by the House Staff, she fluttered up high to the stone ceiling.

She felt her crow's body, tiny and almost insignificant in the entirety of Ilsnare Palace. She had been out flying around the rooftops in the past few days, just 'stretching her wings' . . . although for what cause, she couldn't quite say.

As she flapped herself about the ceiling, she heard a percussive pair of knocks on her chamber door. She allowed herself to drop through the air and, before her talons so much as brushed the floor, she had transformed back into a human . . . albeit a *Magical* one.

She granted entrance to the member of the House Staff and found herself facing off with a rolled-up parchment, tied up with a piece of crimson-coloured silk.

Once she had dismissed the member of the House Staff, she turned her attention down to the parchment. She unrolled it and read the contents.

A missive from the Council of Wisemen.

Asking her to go and meet with them.

For a long while, still tasting the bacon she had had for breakfast at the back of her throat, and feeling a gentle, warming thrum passing through her, sourced from the fireplace over in the corner of her quarters, she couldn't quite square the concept of leaving her cosy surroundings.

She would have to stomp on through the heaps and heaps of snow in order to reach the Galleries of Justice.

And since the sickness had disappeared from the city, the previous levels of bustling activity had returned to the streets of Ilsnare.

Maybe it would be easier if she was to travel as a crow . . .

But, no, in the daytime, and with her going to meet with the Council of Wisemen, she knew that it would be too much of a risk to transform into her crow's body.

She knew well—*by now*—that enchantments were only suitable for use under the cover of night.

And night was still a long way off.

Syre glanced about her quarters, attempting to settle on something which might allow her the excuse not to go. And then, quite without her control, she felt her eyes come to rest on the pile of beaten-up, leather-bound tomes. The ones which she had got hold of at the Palace Library.

She looked over their strange—*twisted*—titles.

The golden embossed lettering all twisting and sneaking about on the spines.

She recalled how, over the past few weeks, she had all but lost her fear of Lou discovering her—of him coming across her reading up on dark magic during the early hours. Although Syre knew that she needed to guard herself against the feeling, she couldn't help but recall what Tineoots had said to her . . . that never before had he experienced magic as *powerful* as her own . . . and, despite this compliment, the only thing which it had served to do was to spur her into extra learning.

And despite telling herself that she wanted to better control her magic, she knew that she was only fooling herself.

No, the truth of the matter was that she wanted to *know* more.

She wanted to be more powerful.

Control could come later.

Syre turned to peer out through the thin glass of the window, down into the courtyard. She eyed the Royal Guards moving sleepily along the battlements. Their wispy-grey uniforms almost caused them to blend in with the sooty-white background; the rooftops all glazed in snow and ice, dirtied by the everyday industry of the city.

What did the Council of Wisemen want with her?

Had they witnessed her victory over Tineoots and wished to pass on their congratulations?

What could they possibly tell her?

What could they possibly *teach* her?

Those words of Tineoots continued to rattle about Syre's mind, almost like a curse; telling her the truth which she had known throughout her life.

That, within her veins, their dwelled the strongest magic, perhaps, on the face of the world.

She would never know unless she explored it further.

It was then that she thought about one of her mother's not-so-subtle, indirect speeches to Syre's father. Her mother would often deliver a lecture superficially intended for Syre and Lou, but really aimed squarely at the chest of their father.

Her mother had spoken to them of the importance of fulfilling potential.

Of, above all else, not allowing talent to go to waste.

She could already tell that Lou was disappearing down *that* particular path—the path of their father who had once been swept up with the greatness of *being* a carpenter, before being unceremoniously *dumped* once the obstacles began to pile up.

Syre, though, had already determined not to be like that at all.

She could—no she *would*—be so much better.

And that only brought her back to thinking of the Council of Wisemen.

Maybe *they* would have some sort of proposal for her.

Something which might speak to the unlimited potential which dwelled in her veins.

But, perhaps more to the point, what did she have to lose by going to meet with the Council of Wisemen?

She was more powerful than them, by far.

Hadn't Tineoots said as much?

WORDS UNSPOKEN

When **Syre reached** the Galleries of Justice, she felt unusually calm.

She moved between the sombre, multi-coloured robes of the Representatives with ease; so much ease that nobody even saw her face.

When she reached the seventh floor, where the Council of Wisemen sat, she brought down the hood of Lou's sheepskin cloak which had come into such great use all throughout this winter, and sniffed at the air.

That same scent of mahogany, a little dust, and musk.

She turned to the dark wood which lined the corridors, and took in the well-polished surfaces. She supposed that the Council of Wisemen was proud of its surroundings; of where they went to work day after day.

She entered the room, her heart fluttering ever so slightly in her chest.

She took in the seven figures; four women, three men.

All of them wore their golden robes over the top of crimson tunics; a detail which, for some reason, tickled Syre this particular afternoon. They all seemed so *puffed-up* . . . almost as if they were full of themselves and their own importance.

She could show them if she wished.

She could show them *all.*

Once Syre had brought the door shut behind her, she felt a touch uneasy, feeling as if they all had their eyes resting over her. It produced a sort of itching sensation just beneath her skin, the same sensation she would get out in the sunlight, with her ice magic protesting against the sun's rays.

Now, though, she needed to hold herself together.

She needed to show them she wasn't afraid.

That there was nothing in their power they could do to stop her.

Syre found herself eyeballing the woman from before, the one who had been so condescending in their previous meeting. She felt her stomach dip and her whole body go slightly rigid. She tried to shift her shoulders, to ease the tension out of her muscles, but—try as she might—she could never manage to get herself completely shot of it.

"Your Majesty," the woman said, her grey hair tidied into a neat bun on the crown of her head, and her eyes a brilliant, liquid blue.

And although the woman's mouth was open for her to continue, Syre decided to cut her off before she could say anything more. "What's your name?" Syre said, deliberately wanting to sound as obtuse as she could manage.

" 'My name', Your Majesty?"

"Yes," Syre replied.

The woman glanced about the Council of Wisemen, and Syre noted some grumbling there too. However, when the woman turned back to look at Syre, she had a grim look of amusement lining her lips. "You really *have* allowed current events to slip, haven't you, ma'am?"

Syre felt her chest tighten.

And she felt the ice magic tingle through her.

Already, she could feel those curses, and hexes, and enchantments rising up to the very surface of her mind. If she so wished it, she could easily spew them out . . . she could show this woman just who *Syre Dorf* really was . . .

But Syre restrained herself to only words, uttered through gritted teeth. "Who *are* you?" she said.

The woman pursed her lips and appeared to consider her answer; putting Syre on guard for the fact that the woman might decide to lie to her; that she might decide to have some sort of *fun* with her.

If the woman did indeed go down that route then Syre would make sure that she would never forget it. She hadn't chosen this situation she found herself in—she'd never *chosen* to become Princess of Shellacnass.

It was just something she had to deal with.

Finally, the woman replied. "My name is Leona," she said, "and I'm the Speaker for the Council of Wisemen."

"The Head of the Council of Wisemen?"

Leona's smile widened. "No," she said, "in accordance with the way in which the Council was derived, there can never be any order of priority for any member of the Council . . . I only express the thoughts which we all discuss." Her smile got wider still. "Think of me as a sort of mouthpiece."

Syre glanced to the other members of the Council. Whenever she caught one of them with her eyes, they looked away; as if they were afraid she'd turned them to frogs, or slugs, or worse, if they only held her eye contact.

She turned back to Leona and wondered just how true of an explanation she had given her. Why *should* Leona tell Syre the truth about anything?

Lou had put this Council in place to govern for him, hadn't he?

She thought back to the parchment which'd brought her here today, and she took a little pleasure in delivering her reply in a somewhat belligerent tone. "What do you want?" Syre said.

Leona continued to stare back into Syre's eyes, and Syre was certain that she could feel the magic bubbling away just beneath the surface of Leona's skin.

For some reason, Syre found herself fantasising about pricking the woman with a pin and seeing just what sort of blood might trickle out.

"We had some enquiries," Leona said.

" 'Enquiries' about *what?*"

"About the nature of what went on at the Palace—about the death of the assassin; of Sheilds Guider; and of Tineoots."

Syre felt her whole body tighten up again.

She found her mind sketching back to what had occurred soon after she'd watched the life leave Tineoots, in the courtyard before her.

The Royal Guards had come to their senses.

One of them had seized her—*quite roughly*—by the arm; and led her away.

As if Tineoots would be any sort of danger now that he was dead.

When one of the Royal Guards had briskly demanded that she return to her quarters, she had informed them of the corpse which was located up there.

She had been told to take refuge in the kitchen . . . although she had, in the end, fled to the Palace Library.

"Yes?" Syre said, tuning back into Leona's question.

Leona held very still, and then said, "We have some concerns following the investigation of the Royal Guards into the death of the assassin, Sheilds Guider, in your quarters."

Syre felt her mind sweep back to those moments, to those heady emotions which'd run through her brain. To the raw power which'd seized hold of her so tightly that she could no longer *think* for herself . . . let alone *control* the magic which flowed through her veins.

The worst part of it all was that she had *enjoyed* every second.

Every second of that raw power—when she had been out of control.

"Go on," Syre said, feeling the ice magic prickle in her veins.

"The wounds to Sheilds Guider were consistent with dark magic." Leona shook her head slightly and then continued, "I mean to say, the sheer brute force of the strike—I cannot quite account for it in all of my knowledge."

"And what knowledge is *that?*" Syre put in.

Leona eyed Syre closely then replied, "Considerable."

Syre held herself still.

She felt her heart beating in her throat.

All at once, she felt as if the seven members of the Council were bearing down on her—as if their gaze was glued to her—as if they were ready to rise up from their seats and hurl hexes in her direction.

She had to be on her guard.

And she would need to respond in kind.

She wouldn't allow them to get the better of her.

She was stronger.

And she was certain of her strength.

"Listen, ma'am," Leona continued, "it's not my place to dabble into the affairs of another mage; and much less a member of the Royal Family. *However*"—she paused sharply, as if giving the word some added gravity—"I shall say this."

Syre felt her ice magic prickling up through her veins, right to the surface of her skin. She could feel it crackling about her fingertips.

So much power.

She could have *so much* power if she only allowed herself to let it go . . . if she allowed herself to get carried away . . . if she allowed herself . . .

"It hasn't escaped my attention," Leona went on, "that you seem somewhat discontented with your role within Ilsnare; and within the Kingdom of Shellacnass as a whole." She met Syre's eye. "Am I correct in my assumption, ma'am?"

The magic was a constant *sting* within Syre's veins now; far more powerful than she ever could've conceived it to be . . . just *who* did they think they were to try and control her, to try and control *magic?*

When she could crush them as simply as bugs beneath a boot heel . . .

From somewhere—somewhere at the back of her mind—Syre channelled into what it was that Leona was saying; about how Syre simply didn't fit here.

And she had to admit that it chimed with her.

Because the truth of the matter was that she *didn't.*

Syre stared back at Leona, feeling as if it would only take a single lapse in her concentration to unleash the magic which was brewing within her.

She would destroy this room.

The Galleries of Justice.

The Crystal City . . .

If she so wished.

They should all be so thankful that she hadn't done so thus far.

But Syre managed to get out a reply. "Yes," she said. "I am *discontented* with my role in Ilsnare."

Leona nodded in return, glanced down at the well-polished table before her for a moment and then looked up again.

Syre could tell that there was no fear in Leona's eyes . . . and Syre wished, more than anything, that there *would* be . . .

"Then listen to my proposal," Leona continued.

Syre stared back.

Her blood continued to prickle through her.

It still took all of her strength to hold it back.

Leona went on, apparently unaware of Syre's inner turmoil. "I propose that you take a Leave of Absence from Ilsnare, from your role as Princess of Shellacnass . . . what would you say to such a proposition?"

Syre still felt the blood swilling through her.

The prickle of it in her veins.

She bunched her fingers into fists.

Felt the sting of her fingernails driven into the tender flesh of her palms.

"I would be interested," Syre replied.

Leona again nodded, as if this was what she expected. "As you are no doubt aware, from our previous discussions, it is the task of the Council of Wisemen—and that of the larger Magical community resident in Ilsnare—to best protect Mortals from harm. At the present time, from the reports . . ." there was a long pause while Leona, apparently, thought of just how much information she might share with Syre ". . . from my *observations*; I believe that it shall be in the best interests of all involved if you were to leave Ilsnare for a time."

There were so many unspoken words within the room; but Syre knew just what they meant to say. That it was the belief of the Council of Wisemen that Syre—or, more exactly, *her dark magic*—might cause great harm to the Crystal City.

And that she was to leave the city behind until such a time as and when she had got it under control.

What they didn't understand, though, was that she didn't *want* to keep it under control.

She wanted power.

She wanted to be as powerful as she could manage.

What did *control* have to do with it?

Syre simply nodded at this statement.

Then she raised her glance to look out through the window, and to the frozen rooftops of the Crystal City.

All catching fire in the sunset.

INTO EXILE

As Syre packed up her travelling bag, she decided that she would take along her brother Lou's sheepskin cloak. She had had it for so long now that he either believed it to be lost, or had come to terms with the truth that it was now—*for better or worse*—in her possession.

She glanced to the many tomes, all piled up, and knew that she couldn't take any of them along with her; not on her travels. But, then again, she had already spent so much time poring over their bruised and beaten pages that she fancied having absorbed a sufficient quantity . . . she had enough to be going on with; perhaps she had already learned all she could from books, maybe what she would need next was a mentor.

Like Lou had had.

Syre thought back on the agreement she had struck with the Council; about how she was to be given a healthy deal of support—*of gold and silver*—to keep her head afloat.

She was to return whenever she saw fit; whenever, it was implied, she had got the dark magic impulses which burned within her under a better sense of control.

And, from the looks of Leona, Syre was fairly certain that she wouldn't be able to pull the wool down over her eyes.

If Syre intended to return to Ilsnare then she would need to control her magic first.

If she intended to return at all.

This morning, Syre had gone about the Throne Room, searching for Lou, but he'd been nowhere to be found. It was just like last night, when she'd returned to the Palace, having been given until sunset the next day to leave the city.

Although she'd been about the Palace searching high and low for Lou, to inform him of the Council's decision, of what had happened, she hadn't been able to locate him . . . and all that despite the various members of the House Staff informing her that he *was* present at the Palace.

When Syre enquired as to whether Sully or Rut were still around the Palace, she was informed that they were not; that they had left behind Ilsnare for some destination unknown.

And without saying goodbye to her.

Syre still had many questions to pose her brother, about where he'd got to on that day when she'd faced off with Tineoots; on why she had been left to face Tineoots alone . . . and she would've liked to reopen a dialogue concerning the Webbing Armoury; would've liked to see Sully and Rut's faces now that they realised Lou's impulse about the danger approaching Ilsnare had been correct.

That Tineoots really had been the threat they'd all expected.

After another lengthy search for Lou, Syre decided that she didn't have the daylight to waste in tracking him down in order to give him some sort of an emotional goodbye.

And surely the Council had already addressed the issue— surely they had informed Lou of their decision to, in effect, banish Syre from Ilsnare.

There could be no other explanation for it.

That Lou was *trying* to avoid her.

Well, he could do whatever he wanted.

He *was* the King of Shellacnass, after all.

With her bags packed, Syre headed down to the stables where she already had a horse waiting; and a stable boy to help her to fasten her belongings to the horse. She thanked the boy and handed him over a coin—*nothing more than a grung*—for his trouble. He reached up and tapped the peak of his cap before disappearing off into the shadows of one of the stables once more.

Up on her horse, Syre breathed in the scent of musk, and manure. It seemed almost a warming odour in the chill of the late-morning air. She felt the bitter bite at her cheeks mitigated by the rising smell. But, soon, this would all be behind her.

She kicked her horse onward, and headed out through the back gates of the Palace for what might very well be the last time.

In the night, much of the snow had melted into black ice, which clung to the cobblestones as an almost hidden menace.

Several times, Syre felt her horse's hoofs slip and slide beneath her, and she prepared to launch herself off its back at a moment's notice . . . that would have been a droll way to start her exile; breaking her back on the cobblestones just outside the Palace; or else to be crushed beneath her own horse's weight.

As she clopped through the streets of Ilsnare, she hunched herself up on the back of her horse.

And she kept the hood of her sheepskin cloak hanging down over her face in order to conceal her features.

Today, given the cold, she didn't look at all suspicious. All the other riders about town, the ones which headed down the Crystal

Causeway—*just as she did now*—were similarly dressed.

Nobody would notice the exiled Princess of Shellacnass.

And Syre was glad.

As she headed for the City Gates, something caught the corner of her eye.

A figure, standing at the entrance to one of the side alleys; one of the many labyrinthine streets which ran all about the city like a network of veins.

Even though the face was in shadow, Syre made out the features.

And she recognised who it was.

Flucknor.

For a second, Syre wondered if he had recognised her, and she thought about simply riding on her way. He wouldn't even know that she had gone. And since he hadn't so much as had the courtesy to inform her *where* he'd disappeared to, she didn't see why she should tell him where she was headed now . . . and then there was the fact that she didn't *know* where she would be headed next . . .

Almost working on a subconscious level, and feeling the steady prickle of the sunlight against her skin, bringing her magical blood to the surface, she turned her horse toward Flucknor.

Before she knew it, she was standing over him, a clear head and shoulders taller.

"Hello," Syre said, deciding to allow the shroud of mystery to slide.

"I heard you're leaving," Flucknor replied.

"Uh-huh," Syre said, and then looked off about the streets, to the cobblestones; and to the snow mounted up against the walls which hadn't yet melted.

There was a long silence between them, and Syre already found herself regretting having stayed behind, having come to say goodbye to Flucknor.

She should've just kept on riding.

That would've been the easiest thing to do.

Syre raised the reins in her grip, and squeezed the leather between her fingers.

She prepared to give the horse a jab of her heels.

To urge him on.

But then Flucknor spoke.

"I think this is the best option," Flucknor replied. "After everything that's happened."

Syre felt her heart chill, and then sink down into her stomach. She stared down at Flucknor, feeling almost as if she might be capable of searing him into cinders where he stood.

She had that sort of power within her . . . she just *knew* it . . .

And then, right when she felt the malice reach its highest point, where she felt that she might be able to do something *impossibly* cruel, and be powerless to stop herself from doing so, she was surprised to feel a smile break out across her lips, and she said, "This world is far more complicated than you believe. If you knew the truth about your passions—about your work with those Creatures; with the *Outcast*—then you'd snap to your senses, and you'd find some other cause to fight for." She jerked her head upward, to indicate his appearance. "Just because we're born into Mortal bodies doesn't mean that we're any less Magical than Creatures; or any less capable of evil."

"Who said anything about evil?" Flucknor replied.

Syre met his gaze for the longest time.

Again, she thought about showing him the extent of her power.

Just what she was capable of.

And she might well have done so if it hadn't been for her horse giving an impatient snort and then stirring its hoofs against the cobblestones.

She tightened her grip on the reins and led him in circles to calm him down, and then she looked back to Flucknor for what she was certain would be the very last time.

"There're two types of Magical being in this world," she said. "Those who hold power, and *choose* not to use it; and then there're those who realise that the world is *theirs* for the taking."

Flucknor stared back up at her, from out of his cloak.

He said nothing in reply.

Not so much as a twitch crossed his features.

He knew how to hide his feelings well—he knew how to *control* his feelings—but that didn't mean that he was stronger than she was.

Just because she *couldn't* hide . . .

As Syre turned her back on him, and kicked her horse into a trot, headed for the pit-black City Gates, she couldn't help but feel the tingle of ice magic passing through her veins.

Because she knew now that she herself had her freedom; that she could be whatever it was that she wanted to be. She no longer had the restrictions.

She didn't have to the play the 'princess' any longer.

Wasn't this all that she had ever wanted?

A DIFFERENT KIND OF SAVIOUR

Lou stood on the ramparts, looking out across the rooftops of Ilsnare.

He stared out across the glass, and saw how the sunrays bounced off the slick surfaces, and how they caught his eyes.

It stung.

Everything about daylight stung him now.

He felt the ice in his veins prickling about his body, refusing to give him any sort of comfort. He knew from experience that the sensation would continue long into the evening; and long after the sun went down tonight.

And the moon came up.

But this affliction was just the burden he had taken on when he had decided to indulge his ice magic. There had been no other way—nobody else to stand up and do what he had *had* to do.

A slight wind was blowing, much warmer.

A southerly breeze coming up from the tropics.

From a place he never imagined seeing with his two eyes.

From all the hobblesmen he had met—the ones who had been presented to him at Court—he had gathered that the waters were an emerald-blue colour, and the currents so still that you could stand in the shallows and peer down at the perfect, sandy seabed.

He recalled those same hobblesmen's descriptions of the sweet taste of coconut, and the fruity smell of bananas growing off the trees; such fruits which Lou had only ever tasted in dried form, from the merchants who brought the produce to sell in Ilsnare marketplace.

If he ever wished to pick a coconut right off the tree—or for that matter a banana—and feel what it was *really* like then he would need to flee this place.

Shun his duties.

But now he felt that Ilsnare—the Kingdom of Shellacnass— needed him more than ever.

As the wind blew about the ramparts, Lou reached out and swept his black cloak behind him, and out of his eye line.

From this point on the ramparts, he could make out the plains; usually endless, rolling green hills all the way to the horizon, but— *today*—they were still speckled with snow.

He wondered if the snow would have all gone by tomorrow; if Ilsnare might have a tiny taste of summer. But he put such thoughts out of his mind almost as soon as they had entered, telling himself that it would only serve to *jink* that eventuality.

In any case, Lou wouldn't be permitted to enjoy any sort of sunshine.

If he was to venture out in the sunlight, he could only imagine the agony which would rack his body.

How it'd feel like a searing-hot blade of a knife was slowly prising his flesh off his bones.

Lou wanted to see her when she left—he wanted to see *Syre* as she trotted out across those plains and away from Ilsnare.

And taking the immediate danger with her.

As Lou stood up on the ramparts, his eyes fixed on the plains just beyond the City Gates, he sensed footsteps behind him. Not with any sort of hearing, not even in the form of vibrations he felt passing through the stone blocks beneath his feet.

No, he could feel the magical forces which surrounded him bend and wane, as dramatic as if the somebody approaching had stepped into a tranquil stream and sent the surface of the water rippling.

Lou didn't break off his stare across the ramparts, not even when the person sidled up beside him, leaned their elbows on the stonework.

Because he knew already who it was.

They had agreed this meeting.

"She's gone," Flucknor said, from Lou's side.

Lou continued to stare out across the plains. He could feel his heart swelling up in his throat. It had been a challenge to stay out of Syre's reach for the past few hours—and, in reality, for the past few weeks—but it had been for the best.

He had already been trying to compartmentalise her within his mind; to mentally prepare himself to let her go.

And to keep himself—*and the entire Kingdom*—from perilous danger.

Lou gave a slight nod, in profile, and he hoped that Flucknor would take it as a satisfactory response. But when Flucknor didn't turn to leave, Lou decided to speak, as dry as his throat was. "Thank you," Lou managed to get out.

Flucknor said nothing in reply.

And neither did he retreat from Lou's side.

Lou realised that Flucknor wanted to *know* . . . he wanted to know *more*.

He supposed that this was the price of keeping a companion; for keeping abreast of events through the Eye—for having used Flucknor in order to monitor Syre's movements, thoughts and feelings; the sorts of things which she would never express to Lou himself.

Lou hadn't enjoyed feeling like a puppet master, directing all of this from the shadows; from the *gloom* of Ilsnare Palace. But it had been the only way he had been able to think of; the only way that he might keep Syre at an arm's length.

Because he knew—and he knew it well—that she would only rise and destroy him if he gave her so much as a chance.

His own sister . . . but she had become corrupt with magic; there was no doubt about that.

Leona, the Speaker of the Council of Wisemen, had confirmed it to him herself.

Lou, of course, had known ever since he had taken the throne—ever since he had become King—that magic dwelled beneath the surface of just about every single everyday activity; not only in the Crystal City, Ilsnare, but in the whole of Shellacnass:

The Crystal Kingdom.

In fact, it had always been the key to protecting the city from danger.

From danger such as Syre.

In the end, it had been Lou's idea to use Tineoots as a sort of stooge; as a means to test out Syre's true nature . . . Tineoots, of course, hadn't been allowed to see the whole picture, but he had become understandably pleased to at least have become the leader of the Eye.

If only in name alone.

And, along with a little foul play, Tineoots had been enough to convince Syre's true nature to shift out from its shell.

For that *darkness* to shine for all who cared to see.

And all of the reports which Flucknor had fed him had turned out to be true . . . goodness, to think of what she had done to that would-be assassin—*to Sheilds Guider*—it made his stomach quiver.

The chill of ice magic rose to the surface of his skin.

There had been no other method, as Lou had learned from mages much more knowledgeable than he, only the threat of death was enough to bring a mage's true nature bubbling up to the surface.

And, in the aftermath, with Leona, and the Council, he had been able to get an objective point of view.

So that it might be possible to strip away all sentiment.

And see the true danger which lurked beneath.

A total success.

The whole operation.

So why did Lou feel so hollow inside?

"What about Rut and Sully?" Flucknor said, breaking the silence between the two of them.

Lou switched his mind back to the present moment.

He had recalled something a fellow mage had once told him— had it been his master Auch'ray?—about how a pair of mages living in close quarters, and at the opposite ends of the light and dark spectrum, would never be able to get along for much time.

So he supposed he should've seen that . . . he should've better anticipated this day's coming.

With his sister so clearly aligned with the dark, and he so clearly aligned with the light.

But, then again, Lou did suppose that he had a Mortal body.

And all the weaknesses which came with it.

He glanced to Flucknor.

He *too* was an ice mage.

Would there come a day when Lou would have to make an equal-ly heart-wrenching decision to cut him off . . . to cast him away?

Perhaps.

If Flucknor, or if Lou himself, were to drift away from the light.

And into darkness.

That would be an end to it.

Lou thought of the question.

He met Flucknor's icy-blue eyes.

"I sent them away," Lou said. "To opposite ends of the Kingdom. Before the day of Tineoots and Sheilds Guider's execution . . . be-fore Syre faced off with the two of them."

Flucknor wrinkled his brow. "Why?"

Lou drew in a heavy breath, right to the bottoms of his lungs. Al-though he had spent the past days and weeks concealing himself in nooks and crannies about the Palace—keeping himself out of sight—he felt weary; almost as if he had been involved in a long journey.

There wouldn't be any more of those for the time being.

Right now, he had to stand and defend the Crystal City.

"To keep the Webbing Armoury safe," Lou finally replied.

" 'The Webbing Armoury'?" Flucknor replied.

Lou prepared a further explanation, the fact that only Sully and Rut—*working together*—held the key to the Webbing Armoury, but he saw that Flucknor already knew this.

He wondered if he had told Flucknor this himself, or if Flucknor had learned the answer through other—*more indirect*—means.

Every day it felt as if Lou's memory was failing him a little more than the previous one.

And yet, within, his magic felt stronger than ever.

More *controlled* than ever.

Lou waited for Flucknor to further question him, to claim that Lou was lying to him—*as he was*—but Flucknor said nothing more.

Lou was certain about one thing, that the secret of what it was that Rut and Sully were up to should be kept well and truly to himself.

Not even his closest ally—the only one who remained—could be trusted with *that* secret.

And he was fully aware of the consequences, as he would often hear Flucknor say:

A secret kept is a burden taken.

"Look!" Flucknor said, extending his arm.

Lou followed his fingertips, felt himself dazed by the sunlight for several seconds before he brought his hand up to shield his eyes. His heart pounded thick and heavy, and he could feel the ice magic itch within his veins. He knew that he wouldn't be able to tolerate being up on the ramparts for much longer; that his ice magic longed to return to the gloomy corridors of the Palace so that it might freeze itself once again.

And, after today, with Syre gone, Lou resolved that he would settle back into a night-time routine.

Lou scoured the plains, but no matter how hard he looked, he couldn't catch sight of a horse.

Perhaps his eyes were failing him as badly as his memory.

Finally, Lou let go of his pride, and said, "Where? Where is she?"

"There," Flucknor said, still extending his fingers in the apparent direction of Syre.

Lou screwed up his eyes, straining his focus as hard as he dared.

He realised that Flucknor was indicating the sky.

The sky just above the plains.

Finally, Lou caught sight of her.

Of that sooty, black spot on the otherwise clear blue sky.

A *crow.*

Flapping her way up into the sky.

And away from the City Walls.

Soaring off into the distance.

Lou stood there for what felt like hours, clutching the stone of the ramparts, feeling all the blood draining from his hands as he gripped.

In the end, it was only when Flucknor touched him on the shoulder, gave him a faint smile, and said, "Come on, Your Majesty, she's gone," that Lou realised that—*really*—she had gone.

That she'd slipped from sight.

Lou felt as if he was rooted to the spot, as if he would forever stare out across the stone ramparts and to the now-vacant sky.

Where he had last seen Syre.

Something deep within snapped.

Told him that now was the time.

That his kingdom needed him.

And that it was time to move on.

To be the one they all needed.

The man they all looked up to.

And even as he felt his ice magic slicing him open from the inside, he paced strong and confident along the ramparts, with Flucknor at his side, and he knew that—as before—the Crystal City would depend on magic to stay safe.

His magic.

AUTHOR'S NOTE

Thank you for picking up and (hopefully!) enjoying one of my stories.

When it comes to reaching readers in the modern era, reviews mean everything to authors. This is where you can help out. If you have a spare moment I would really appreciate it if you could leave an (honest!) review on the sales page for this title.

To hear about my latest releases — and to get your hands on some free fiction (!) — you can sign up for my newsletter: www.raymondsflex.com/readers

Thank you so much for reading!

Raymond S Flex

ABOUT THE AUTHOR

Raymond S Flex:

Science fiction. Fantasy. And everything in between!

Among tales of laser blasters, crazed sprites and diabolically minded executives sits the Crystal Kingdom epic fantasy series. Join Louson Dorf — and a burgeoning cast of characters — as he strives to piece his crumbling world back together again.

Get free fiction, notification of the latest releases, and more, when you join Raymond S Flex's mailing list: www.raymondsflex.com/readers

COMPLIMENTARY
DIGITAL EDITION

A complimentary digital edition is
included with this book.

To download your epub, mobi & PDF
versions of this book, please navigate to
www.dibbooks.com/digital-editions/ and when
prompted for a password enter the following:

needle

books

www.ingramcontent.com/pod-product-compliance
Lightning Source LLC
Chambersburg PA
CBHW021003260626
47169CB00006B/1927